"You can't deny me the right to my son!"

Ashley's plea was accompanied by her hand on his arm, gripping the taut muscles. It was more than seven years since she had touched Alain....

"Ashley!" he grated savagely. "Please get away from me before I am compelled to deliver the punishment I should have administered years ago!"

She didn't move away. Suddenly she sensed that for all his anger and threats he wasn't as indifferent to her as he would like her to believe.

Was it possible, she asked herself incredulously, that after all these years he had some regrets for the pain and misunderstandings of the past? But no, that wasn't like Alain. He had always been so controlled, so remote from any weaknesses. Except when he had been in her arms....

ANNE MATHER
is also the author of these

Harlequin Presents

and these
Harlequin Romances

Many of these titles are available at your local bookseller.

For a free catalogue listing all available Harlequin Romances and Harlequin Presents, send your name and address to:

HARLEQUIN READER SERVICE
1440 South Priest Drive, Tempe, AZ 85281
Canadian address: Stratford, Ontario N5A 6W2

ANNE MATHER

castles of sand

Harlequin Books

TORONTO • LONDON • LOS ANGELES • AMSTERDAM
SYDNEY • HAMBURG • PARIS • STOCKHOLM • ATHENS • TOKYO

Harlequin Presents edition published August 1981
ISBN 0-373-10449-9

Original hardcover edition published in 1981
by Mills & Boon Limited

CHAPTER ONE

THE room was quiet. Even though it was only a stone's throw from the busy heart of London's West End, the school buildings seldom allowed more than the steady hum of traffic to invade their thick walls, and Kingsley Square was a sequestered backwater, secure from the noise and confusion scarcely half a mile away. Sitting at her desk, with a pile of crisp new exercise books in front of her, Ashley could not have wished for more private surroundings to bear the shock she had just experienced, and yet it still left her shaking and incapable of coherent thought.

She looked at the register of names in front of her, and ran a trembling finger down the column. Devlin, Fredericks—perhaps she had been mistaken—but no, there it was again, *Gauthier*, Hussein Gauthier, there was no mistake. And it was not such a common name either. Surely, *surely*, there could not be two seven-year-old boys called Hussein Gauthier.

She did not often take a drink, but right now Ashley felt she could do with one. Her mouth felt dry, and her head was spinning, and although she knew there were other matters to be taken into consideration, all she could think of was that she was expected to have the boy in her form for a whole year!

It couldn't be done. Her initial reactions were all negative. She would not—she *could* not—be expected to teach him; not in the present circumstances. It was too much to ask of anyone, any woman, at least. How could it have happened? What cruel twist of fate had brought the boy to this school, out of all the schools that could have been chosen? It was intolerable, it was unkind, it was *inhuman*!

Ashley got up jerkily from her desk, pushing back her chair so abruptly, it almost fell over, and rocked dangerously on its back legs. But it steadied itself, as Ashley tried to do, before stepping down from the small dais and walking determinedly towards the door.

Outside, the polished wooden blocks of the floor of the corridor stretched ahead of her, the walls lined with portraits of past headmasters of Brede School. Between the portraits, half glass doors opened into other classrooms and activity rooms, empty until tomorrow when the school re-opened after the summer recess. Ashley herself had only come in that morning to acclimatise herself to her surroundings again, and to run a casual eye over the new pupils she was to have charge of. She had been away, staying with some friends in Yorkshire, enjoying the unaccustomed freedom from books and learning, joining in the work of the farm, where she had spent the last two months. The Armstrongs had always been like her own family to her. She and Lucy Armstrong had met at university, and since then, apart from those disastrous months she had spent with Hassan, she had remained in regular contact with them. As she had no parents of her own, there had been many occasions when she had been grateful for their support, and at this very moment she would have welcomed Mr Armstrong's practical common sense.

The corridor emerged on to a railed landing, overlooking the entrance hall below. The school had originally been formed in the eighteenth century by linking together two town houses, and although the buildings had been added to since that time, the atmosphere of a close community remained. There were lots of halls and curiously winding staircases, and low beams to catch the unwary, but as the boys it accommodated were only five to thirteen years of age, it seldom troubled them. It was a small school, only a hundred and fifty pupils, but its record was excellent, and its results ensured a permanent register of pupils waiting to receive a place.

As she hurried down the stairs, Ashley wondered how Hussein had been admitted. Had his name been entered since his birth, as many of the boys' names had, or had someone in authority pulled some strings? She could hardly believe the former, and although the latter seemed more likely, what unknowing chance had prompted Alain to choose *this* school?

Malcolm Henley, the present headmaster of Brede School, had his study on the ground floor, in a room which had once been used as a reception parlour. It was not a large room, but the ceiling was high, and the bookshelves that lined the walls drew one's eyes upwards rather than pointing to its limited proportions. It was a comfortable room, a masculine room, with rather austere furnishings and fittings, but Ashley had always felt at ease here, and during the five years she had been working in the school, she and Malcolm had become close friends.

Now, she knocked at the door, and having been bidden to enter, stepped on to the worn brown carpet. Malcolm had been seated at his desk, but at her entrance he rose politely to his feet, and with a warm smile came round the desk to greet her.

'Well, Ashley,' he said, as she closed the door behind her. 'Have you satisfied yourself that everything is as you left it?'

Ashley forced a faint smile. 'Yes. Yes, I've done that,' she answered, withdrawing her hand from his enthusiastic hold. 'And—and I checked over the new register of pupils.'

Malcolm nodded, pulling his pipe out of his pocket, and examining the bowl with a knowing eye. 'You'll see you've got fifteen boys this year,' he remarked, searching his pockets for some matches. 'I've agreed to take on an extra pupil, one who is slightly older than we usually take them, but an intelligent boy for all that, or so I believe.'

'Hussein Gauthier,' put in Ashley tightly, and Malcolm acknowledged this as he struck a match.

'Gauthier, yes, that is the boy's name,' he agreed, smiling as he dropped the spent match into the already overflowing ashtray. Then a look of mild concern crossed his lined, yet still handsome, face. 'Is something wrong, Ashley? You look—disturbed.'

Ashley indicated the chair at the opposite side of the desk. 'May I sit down?'

'Of course.' Malcolm walked to resume his seat. 'Need you ask?' He frowned. 'You're not ill, are you?'

'Physically, you mean?' suggested Ashley, a vaguely hysterical note lurking in her voice. 'No. No, Malcolm, I'm not ill. At least, not in any way that you can see.'

Malcolm rested his elbows on the desk and regarded her thoughtfully across its littered width. 'You are upset, aren't you? What is it? Is there anything I can do?'

Ashley lay back in the worn leather armchair and wished desperately that there was. But she didn't see what anyone could do—except herself. She and Malcolm had never discussed her past. Oh, he knew she had been married, and that her husband had died within a few days of that marriage, but that was all. She had never discussed his identity, or their relationship, and as she had reverted to her maiden name of Gilbert, the rest of the staff were no wiser.

'Would you like a drink?'

Malcolm indicated the decanter on the filing cabinet by the window, but Ashley shook her head. 'It's only eleven o'clock,' she protested, and Malcolm shrugged his shoulders.

'Perhaps you need one,' he suggested, and remembering her own thoughts of only a few minutes ago, Ashley acquiesced. Maybe it would be easier to say what she had to say with a little dutch courage inside her. She didn't honestly know what she was going to say, but something had to be said, that was certain.

With a glass containing a measure of Scotch whisky in her hand, Ashley strove to find a way to explain herself. 'I—I have to offer you my resignation,' she said, clearing her throat as Malcolm stared at her aghast. 'I—I'm sorry. I know it's an awkward time for you, the beginning of term and everything, but—I—I'm sorry.'

She buried her nose in the glass as Malcolm digested what she had just told him. Characteristically, he did not immediately deny her claim, but sat there quietly smoking his pipe, watching her with the same assessing intentness, with which he appraised the boys.

'I assume you do intend to tell me why you've come to this decision,' he said at last, when Ashley had choked over the raw alcohol and set her eyes streaming. 'You do realise that I care about you, and am concerned about you, and that whatever it is that's troubling you is better shared?'

Ashley expelled her breath shakily. 'You're very kind, Malcolm, but——'

'I'm not kind!' he retorted briefly. 'I'm concerned. That's a completely different thing.'

Ashley sighed. Malcom was kind, whatever he said. Kind, and understanding, and had she never known another kind of loving she might easily have succumbed to his affectionate attentions. But when she first came to Brede School to work, she had still been raw from her experiences with the Gauthiers, and she had made it plain that so far as men were concerned she preferred them to keep their distance. In consequence, the association which had developed over the years between her and Malcolm was compounded of a mutual liking and respect, and if, as a bachelor of almost forty years, Malcolm still hoped for a closer relationship, Ashley was not to blame. Nevertheless she did not want to hurt him, and she was loath to destroy what she had built up without due cause.

'I have to leave,' she said now, choosing her words with care. 'Something—something's happened. I—I can't stay on.'

Malcolm tapped out his pipe in the ashtray, spilling smouldering shreds of tobacco over the scarred surface of his desk, so that he had to rescue several papers from ignition. Then, turning an unusually taut gaze on Ashley, he said:

'Why? Why can't you? You seemed perfectly all right when you arrived this morning. Why, we waved to one another across the quadrangle. For heaven's sake, if you were thinking of leaving, why didn't you warn me then?'

Ashley shook her head, looking down into her glass, and with sudden perception Malcolm brought his fist down hard upon the desk. 'I have it!' he exclaimed. 'You weren't thinking of leaving then, were you? It's something else. Something that's happened this morning. Something to do with this new form you're taking——'

'No——' began Ashley, realising he was closing on the truth, but Malcolm wasn't listening to her.

'It must have to do with the boy,' he finished at last. 'What was his name? Gauthier—Hussein Gauthier! Of course,' this as Ashley turned a stricken face towards him. 'Why didn't I realise it before? You identified him immediately, as soon as I mentioned a new boy. I should have connected the two things sooner, only I was more concerned about you.'

Ashley set down her scarcely-touched glass with a weary hand. What was the point of denying it any longer? she thought. Malcolm was no fool. He could demand a satisfactory explanation, he deserved a satisfactory explanation. So why pretend she could just leave here without arousing his suspicions?

'Well?' he was asking now. 'I am right, aren't I? It's the boy Gauthier who's upset you. Why? What's he to you? Do you know him? Do you know his family? Ashley, I mean to find out, so you might as well be honest with me.'

Ashley inclined her head. 'He's my son,' she said simply, folding her hands in her lap. 'Hussein—*Andrew*—Gauthier is my son.'

Malcolm's astonishment was not contrived. A look of stunned disbelief crossed his features and remained there. He was evidently shaken, and who could blame him? she thought bleakly. She had never, at any time, mentioned that she had had a child.

'Don't you think that statement deserves some explanation?' he ventured at last, thrusting his pipe back into his pocket with somewhat unsteady haste. 'You told me you'd been married, that your husband was dead. But—but not that—that there were children!'

'There were no *children*,' retorted Ashley wearily. 'Only one child. And—and as I never saw him, I never felt as if he was mine.'

'But you must have done!' Malcolm stared at her. 'Ashley, a woman always cares about her children.'

'Not all women,' corrected Ashley tautly, controlling her emotions with great difficulty. 'But you're right about me, as it happens. I did care. At least, in the beginning.'

Malcolm shook his head. 'You mean to tell me you've never even *seen* this boy?'

'That's right.'

'But how—why? How did it happen?'

Ashley sighed. 'It's a long story, Malcolm——'

'And don't you think I deserve to hear it?'

Ashley pressed her lips together. 'Perhaps. Perhaps you do—I don't know. Oh, Malcolm, what am I going to do?'

Malcolm got up from his chair and came round to her, perching on the side of his desk and looking down at her with compassionate eyes. 'I meant what I said, you know. A trouble shared can help one to see it in its right perspective. Perhaps if you talked to me——'

'I can't teach my own son!' declared Ashley emotively. 'I can't, Malcolm. I can't!'

'I see there's a problem,' said Malcolm levelly, but as she would have protested again, he held up one hand. 'Wait,' he said. 'Hear me out. This is something we have to talk about.'

Ashley made a helpless gesture. 'What is there to say? It's an impossible situation.'

'First of all, I want you to tell me why you haven't seen—Hussein—all these years.' He frowned. 'And why you added the name Andrew. I don't recall the boy having that name.'

'He doesn't.' Ashley moved her shoulders wearily. 'That was my name for him. I called him Andrew. I—I refused to have a son of mine with only an Arab name.'

Malcolm nodded. 'All right, I understand that. But I had no idea your husband was an Arab. I imagined he was someone you'd met in England.'

'I did meet him in England,' said Ashley flatly. 'I—I met his brother at—at the home of a girl I got to know at university. And—and through him, I got to know Hassan.'

'I see.' Malcolm digested this. 'So you know his family?'

'I—knew his brother,' Ashley corrected tightly.

Malcolm sighed. 'Yet you were married. You had a child!'

'I lived in London,' Ashley explained. 'Hassan had been working here before we got married.'

'Of course.' Malcolm slapped his hand to his knee. 'The Gauthiers are in oil and shipping, aren't they?' He gave her a strange look. 'Ashley, did you realise what a wealthy family you were marrying into?'

Ashley's long lashes veiled her expression. 'Yes, I realised it,' she replied dully. 'You might say—that was why I married Hassan.'

'Ashley!'

'Well——' she tilted her gaze up to him, her green eyes dark and haunted, 'I wouldn't be the first girl to admit that. It's true. I was pregnant, you see.'

'Oh, my dear!' Malcolm made a sound of sympathy. 'And you were—how old?'

'Eighteen,' she answered blankly. 'In my first year at the college.' She gave a tight smile. 'I was very naïve.'

Malcolm hesitated. 'But he did marry you. Some men—well, you know what I mean.'

'Oh, yes,' Ashley assented, 'I know what you mean. But Hassan—always got what he wanted, and he wanted me.'

She said it without conceit, and Malcolm watched her closely. 'You're still bitter.'

Ashley's smile was self-derisive. 'Yes.'

'Your husband dying so soon after the wedding—that must have been a great shock to you.'

Ashley's expression hardened. 'Yes.'

'They—his family—they wouldn't let you keep the boy?'

Ashley bent her head. 'I'd really rather not talk about it.'

'Which means I'm right, doesn't it?'

'Malcolm, you don't understand.'

'What don't I understand?'

Ashley sighed. 'Hassan died the day after the wedding——'

'So?'

'——and his family blamed me!'

Malcolm stared at her. 'Why?'

Ashley turned her head away. 'Oh, Malcolm, don't make me go into all the details. Let it be enough that they thought they had grounds for thinking that.'

'But it wasn't true?'

Ashley looked at him with tortured eyes. 'No, it wasn't true.'

'And later, when they found out you were pregnant?'

Ashley hunched her shoulders. 'We were estranged. I'd gone back to college. When—when—Hassan's brother found out, he gave me a choice of alternatives.' Her lips twisted. 'Either I handed over the child when he was born, and allowed them to bring him up in the way he deserved, or he would wait until the child was older and then fight for him through the courts.' She expelled her breath unsteadily. 'I wanted to do that, to keep him, and care for him, but how could I? I had no money of my own, and I wanted nothing from the Gauthiers. And—and I knew Alain meant what he said. He would have taken Andrew from me, by one means or another.' She bit hard on her lips to prevent them from trembling, then added tautly: 'You read about these things every day. Babies, children—snatched from this country, and taken to live with their fathers in some foreign place. Alain could have done that, he *would* have done that, I know. And how much harder it would have been for me to lose him after I'd learned to love him . . .'

She avoided Malcolm's eyes as she said this. There were other reasons why she had let the boy go, but she had no intention of revealing them. She had told him too much already, more than she had told anyone, except the

Armstrongs, without whom she might never have recovered from that traumatic experience. But it had been
over. There had even been days when she had not
thought about him at all. And now to find she was not to
be allowed to forget it was the cruellest blow of all.

'Alain?' said Malcolm now. 'This, I assume, is Hassan's
brother.'

'Yes.'

'But their names are dissimilar. And Gauthier—that's
not an Arab name.

'No.' Ashley cleared her throat again. 'There's—there's
French ancestry somewhere in their history, and—and
Alain's mother was French, actually. She—she was his
father's second wife.'

Malcolm's eyes narrowed. 'You mean your husband
and his brother had different mothers?'

'That's right.'

'Hassan—your husband—his mother died?'

'No.' Ashley spoke tautly. 'So far as I know, she's still
alive. Prince—Prince Ahmed is a Moslem.'

Malcolm was amazed. 'I see.'

Ashley had had enough of this. Pushing back her chair,
she got to her feet, moving away from Malcolm and stiffening her spine. 'So you see,' she said, endeavouring to
speak calmly, 'my remaining here is—is quite out of the
question. I shall look——'

'Wait. Wait!' Malcolm slid off the desk and stood
facing her impotently, balling his hand into a fist, and
pressing it into his palm. 'Ashley, there must be something I can do, some way I can persuade you to change
your mind.' He paced restlessly across the floor. 'If I were
to transfer him to another class—transfer you to another
class——'

Ashley shook her head. 'You couldn't do that, Malcolm. He's—seven. He should be with seven-year-olds.'

'But there's no reason why you shouldn't take another
form,' Malcolm pointed out recklessly. 'If I speak to
Harry Rogers——'

Ashley turned away. 'He'd still be in the school.'

'But——' Malcolm made a sound of frustration, 'you wouldn't know him. You need never see him. He would be just another boy——'

'You're asking a lot,' Ashley exclaimed, glancing at him over her shoulder. 'Could you do it? Could you work here, knowing your son was in the school and didn't know you?'

Malcolm had the grace to look disconcerted. 'I don't know.'

'I don't think you could,' said Ashley steadily. 'I don't think anyone could.'

'Well, you must give me time to think, to make arrangements,' Malcolm exhorted desperately. 'Tomorrow the boarders return, and the day after that school reopens. You can't abandon me without notice, Ashley.'

Ashley held up her head. 'How much notice do you want?'

'Oh, I don't know. A month is usual. A term would be better.'

'And in my case?'

Malcolm sighed. 'Two weeks?' he ventured tentatively.

'*Two weeks!*' Ashley sucked in her breath. 'Malcolm——'

'I'll transfer you. I'll let Rogers take your form. Who knows, you may change your mind.'

'I won't.' Ashley was very definite about that. But she managed to maintain a semblance of composure as she added: 'I'll submit my written resignation this afternoon. And I'll transfer my things to Room 1A.'

Malcolm made a baffled gesture. 'Won't you at least think about this, Ashley? You've been here five years!'

'I know.' Ashley moved towards the door. 'And they've been good years. But you must see, I have to do this.'

Eventually he let her go, but she knew he was not entirely satisfied that she was determined. He still held out hopes that she might change her mind, while Ashley knew that nothing he said or did could alter her decision. She would be sad to leave Brede School. She had been happy here, or at least, she had been content. Now she

was lost and uncertain, with the unwelcome knowledge
that it was not going to be easy to find another post. It
was the wrong time of the year, and she could only hope
that there was someone else, like her, who suddenly found
her present position intolerable.

But even as these thoughts occurred to her, they were
superseded by others. Andrew was going to be living in
England, in *London*, and unless she took a post out of the
capital, he would always be only a few miles away. Her
small flat in Kilburn was only a bus ride from the school.
She could make it there in less than half an hour. Could
she bear to go on living within breathing distance of her
son?

She hurried along the corridor from Malcolm's study
with a feeling of impending disaster weighing down on
her. Why, oh, why had Alain chosen to send the boy back
to England to be educated? She would never have expected it of him. The United States, perhaps, but not
England. Not after everything that had happened.

And then again, she argued, why not? Both Alain and
Hassan had been educated in England. Why should she
have imagined anything less would be good enough for
Andrew? He was a Gauthier. And unless Alain had married and produced a son, the only heir to his grandfather's fortune.

Ashley's stomach churned. Alain could have married,
she acknowledged, but the thought still had the power to
leave her weak. It was not fair, she thought, that one man
should wield so much power over her, particularly when
he regarded her as an inferior being, a nonentity, something to be trampled on. And it was ironic that history
should have appeared to have reversed itself. Prince
Ahmed had married Alain's mother after his first wife,
Princess Izmay, had produced a series of daughters. But,
within a year of Alain being born, she had borne him a
son, Hassan, thus ensuring the line of succession. Now
Alain's brother had succeeded in marrying before him,
and the son Ashley had had was heir to Prince Ahmed.

In the entrance hall she paused, looking about her

almost with a sense of bereavement. This school had come to mean a lot to her. She knew many of the boys, as they had passed through her form on their way to the middle school. She was popular with them, and being young herself could understand their problems better than some of the older masters. She and the biology mistress were the only female tutors on the staff, and she had begun to regard it less like a job and more like a vocation. She had never thought of marrying again, and these boys had become her family. Brought up by an elderly aunt, without either brothers or sisters of her own, she had welcomed their friendship and their confidences, and she dreaded the thought of beginning again with strangers.

The doorbell rang behind her, and she turned automatically, going to open it without hesitation. She guessed it might be the launderers or the caterers, or even the firm of contractors who had been redecorating the dormitories, and making minor repairs, and she flung the door wide, glad of the diversion. But the man and the boy who stood outside the door were not tradespeople at all, and Ashley's jaw sagged in horror as she perceived their identity.

The man, too, looked taken aback at her appearance, but with the assurance that came from his position he recovered more quickly, hiding his real feelings behind a mask of courtesy. As she struggled to evade the encroaching wave of blackness that threatened to engulf her, he gathered his composure and assumed a polite expression, and she was left to gaze at the boy, as if she was afraid he might disappear in a cloud of smoke.

She couldn't believe it. After all these years, she simply couldn't believe it, and her knees shook abominably as she hung desperately on to the door handle. The amazing thing was, he even looked like her, although he had his father's dark hair and skin. But the green eyes were hers, and so too was the straight nose, and the generous mouth was parted slightly, as if aware of some irregularity here.

'Miss—Miss Gilbert, is it not?' Just by the momentary hesitation did Alain betray his agitation, and Ashley dragged her gaze from the boy's tall slim figure to the man's tautly controlled features.

'P-Prince Alain,' she acknowledged, bowing her head. 'Wh-what can I do for you?'

Alain glanced about him half impatiently, as if seeking deliverance. A tall lean man, with straight dark hair, and just the slightest crook in his nose, where it had once been broken in a boyish fight, he had changed little over the years, she thought. He was, she knew, in his early thirties now, and although the lines in his face were more deeply carved than they had been, he was still the most disturbing man she had ever encountered. In an immaculately-cut European suit, he looked cool and businesslike, but she also knew he looked equally well in a loose flowing burnous or the tunic-like djellaba he had worn about his apartment. The *apartment*! Her tongue clove to the dry roof of her mouth. Why did she have to think of that now?

Alain fixed her with a steely gaze, and then spoke, almost with reluctance. 'I wish to speak with a Monsieur Henley,' he declared, his deep voice harsher than she remembered. 'He is the headmaster here, is he not? Will you please tell him I am here?'

Just like that, thought Ashley bitterly. Within the space of a few moments, he had accepted her presence in the school and dismissed it, and was already issuing his orders. He did not ask how she was; he did not ask what she was doing here; he did not care how she might be feeling, having just seen her son for the first, and possibly *only*, time in her life. Without sensitivity or emotion, he expected her to do his bidding, and ignore the deeper ravages of time and circumstance.

Her eyes moved to the boy again, searching his face eagerly, hungrily, seeking some recognition from him, even though she knew such a thing was impossible. The boy did not know her. He had probably not been told of her existence. And of a certainty, his uncle would never reveal her identity.

Yet, as if aware of the intentness of her gaze, Andrew

responded, his mouth tilting at the corners to form a smile, a smile that entered his eyes and caused them to twinkle with evident humour. He smiled at her, shyly but warmly, and her heart palpitated wildly at this evidence of his amusement. Ashley could feel the tears pricking at the back of her eyes, she could sense the unspoken communication between them; and she knew an almost uncontrollable impulse to put her arms around him and hold him close . . .

'Mr Henley, *mademoiselle*?' Alain did not move, but the barrier his words erected was an almost physical thing. 'He is here, is he not?'

'What? Oh! Oh, yes. Yes, of course.'

Foolishly, Ashley stepped backward, her eyes still on the boy, still shaking with the emotions he had aroused in her. He was so handsome, she thought, so *beautiful*! And he was *hers*! Her son! Hers and——

'Will you give Mr Henley my message?'

Alain's voice had hardened, and as she dragged her eyes to him once again she flinched beneath the withering contempt of his gaze. Of course, she thought bitterly, he must know how she was feeling, but what satisfaction was he getting from torturing her in this way?

Shaking her head, she tried to recover some perspective. He was here—*they* were here—to see Malcolm, and somehow she had to accept that this encounter was an accident, nothing more, a cruel accident, for which none of them was to blame. It was not a deliberate attempt to wound her, to crucify her with images of what might have been. Alain must be as shocked as she was, but she knew well his capacity to hide his true feelings.

'I—er—I'll get someone to take you to Mr Henley,' she said huskily, knowing she could not do it herself. Not now. Not when Malcolm knew! It would be just too much for her to bear.

As they stepped into the hall she looked about her desperately, praying for a friendly face, and was rewarded when Mr Norris, the elderly caretaker, came trudging down the stairs.

'Oh, Mr Norris,' she exclaimed in relief. 'Mr—er—this gentleman wishes to see Mr Henley. Do you think you could show him the way to Miss Langley's office? She—she'll see if Mr Henley is free.'

'Very well, Miss Gilbert.' Mr Norris smiled. He liked the young English mistress. She was quiet and unassuming, and she wasn't always complaining when the lights fused or the radiators persistently remained cold. 'If you'll follow me, Mr—er——?

'Gauthier,' inserted Alain without expression, shunning his title. 'Thank you.'

His thanks encompassed both of them, but Ashley was scarcely paying attention. She was looking at Andrew again, imprinting his likeness in her mind, creating an image for all the empty years ahead of her, holding it there with a persistence born of desperation. If only, she thought, as he started obediently after Mr Norris, *if only* . . .

'Do not even think of it,' Alain's harsh voice decreed, in a tone low enough for only her to hear. 'He is not your son. He is Hassan's. He will never be told that his mother caused his father to take his own life!'

CHAPTER TWO

ASHLEY arrived back at her flat in a state of extreme nervous exhaustion. She had a sense of unreality, too, as if what had happened was just some awful nightmare, from which she must soon awaken. But although she might wish otherwise, the feelings fermenting inside her were not imaginary, nor was the raw vulnerability of her emotions. She felt exposed and defenceless, powerless in the face of such a potent adversary, and no amount of objective thinking or cold self-analysis could spare her the agony of losing her son for the second time.

As she ground the beans and filled the coffee percolator, all without any conscious thought, she thought how incredible it was that she should have allowed the Gauthiers to take him without a fight. He was *her* son. She was his mother. She had the most elemental right in the world to look after him, and care for him, so why had she let him go so easily?

Clattering a cup into a saucer, she knew she did not have to think hard to find the answer. It was because of Alain she had let him go, because of Alain she had not put up a fight; and because of Alain she was now in this deplorable position.

Leaving the coffee to bubble, she went into the main room of the flat. This was a comfortably-sized living room, with an L-shaped alcove accommodating a round dining table and four chairs. It had taken her three years to graduate to this standard of living, from a room in a boarding house, via a bedsitter, to this two-bedroomed apartment, with kitchen and bath. With care, and careful saving, she had finally succeeded in furnishing it to her liking, and she looked round now at the green velvet chairs and yellow-patterned carpet, in a desperate search for reassurance. But all she could see was a boy's smiling face, framed by straight dark hair, and a man's grim, forbidding countenance.

In an effort to escape the futility of her thoughts, she hurried into her bedroom, unbuttoning the skirt and blouse she had worn to go to school and donning instead a pair of yellow baggy pants and a brown and green striped smock. Then she loosened her hair from its confining knot so that it spilled like honey-coloured silk below her shoulders. As she brushed its silken length, she realised it was an unnecessary vanity. It would be far more sensible to have it cut, and keep it in one of the short modern styles, which were so flattering to the girls of her acquaintance. But somehow it was a link with the past, an unconscious one to be sure, and only now did she realise that Alain's influence still reached out to her.

The percolator was bubbling merrily when she went back into the kitchen, and after pouring herself a cup of coffee she carried it into the living room. It was after two o'clock, she realised with a pang, but she wasn't hungry, and she determinedly picked up the daily paper and tried to interest herself in the national news. But the events of the morning persisted in intruding, and eventually she gave it up to recapture those moments when Andrew had smiled at her. She allowed herself the pleasure of wondering what he would have done if she had taken him in her arms and told him who she was. How would he have reacted? Would he have been pleased or apprehensive, glad or sorry? Would he have believed her? Or would he have thought she was some crazy lady, claiming a relationship that was totally alien to him? He had been brought up by the Gauthiers. It was a predominantly Moslem household. How could he ever identify with her, particularly after all this time?

Her coffee cooled as the realities of the situation dispelled her momentary euphoria. They were from different cultures, different civilisations. From an early age he would have been taught to regard women as secondary beings, created for man's enjoyment and little else, expected always to defer to their masters, and obedient to

their wishes. He would know that his grandfather had
two wives, and even if Alain's beliefs had been in opposition to his father's, who was to say what those beliefs were
now, or whether he too had not adopted the sexual
morals of the rest of his family.

Her temples began to throb as she remained there on
the couch, her knees drawn up under her, her head resting wearily against the soft cushions. Who would have
dreamed when she awakened that morning that by
lunchtime she would have suffered such a dramatic
upheaval? She had made her life here, such as it was. She
had made friends, she had a good job. Yet in the space of
a morning it had all been destroyed, and she was left
without peace or tranquillity, or *hope*.

She thrust the still full coffee cup on to the low table
beside her and stretched her legs. Somehow she had to
forget what had happened, she told herself severely. She
had lived seven years without seeing her son; she might
have to live another fifty years without doing so. Of
course, there was always the chance that when Andrew
got older he might start asking questions his grandfather
and his uncle would not be able to answer, and then he
might come looking for her himself. But that was an unlikely expectation to say the least, when for all she knew,
Alain might have told him she was dead.

She closed her eyes against such a final denigration,
then opened them again when someone knocked at her
door. It was a peremptory tattoo, unlike her neighbour's
usual tap, but she couldn't think of anyone other than
Mrs Forest who might call at this time of day.

'Coming,' she called, sliding off the couch, and pad-
ding barefoot to the door. 'You startled me,' she was
adding, as she lifted the latch, and then fell back in
dismay when she recognised her visitor. 'You!' she
breathed, pressing a hand to her throat. 'Wh-what do
you want? Why have you come here?'

'An unnecessary question,' remarked Alain flatly,
stepping past her without invitation. 'Why else would
I come here, except to see you? Can you honestly say

you did not expect me?'

'Yes!' Ashley strove for breath. 'Yes,' she repeated. 'I can honestly say that. Wh-why have you come here? Why should you want to see me?'

Alain turned in the centre of the floor, dark and forbidding in his charcoal grey attire. 'Close the door, will you?' he directed, flicking a careless hand, on the little finger of which a dragon's eye ruby glinted balefully. 'I do not propose to speak with you in sight and hearing of a crowd of inquisitive tenants.'

'You flatter yourself,' returned Ashley tensely, making no move to obey him. 'And why should I allow you into my apartment? We—we have nothing to say to one another.'

'I disagree,' Alain argued smoothly, and with an arbitrary gesture he crossed the floor to her side, rescuing the handle of the door from her grasp and closing it firmly with a definite click.

'You have no right to do this,' Ashley protested, gazing up at him tremulously, but Alain did not acknowledge her indignation. As she struggled to compose herself, he returned to his position in the centre of the floor and suggested she take a seat.

'This is my flat,' Ashley declared, endeavouring to hide the tremor in her voice. 'I'll decide when or if I sit down, not you!'

'As you wish.' Alain's mouth thinned. 'You were always an argumentative creature. But what I have to say may make you change your mind, so be warned.'

Ashley took a deep breath. 'You—you have a nerve, coming here, trying to tell me how to behave——'

'I do not propose to get involved in futile discussions of that sort,' he interrupted her bleakly. 'You and I have known one another too long to be in any doubt as to one another's character, and——'

'We *never* knew one another!' Ashley choked bitterly. 'You didn't know me, and it's certain I never knew you!'

'Please try not to be emotional,' Alain advised her briefly, folding his arms across the waist-coated expanse of his chest. 'I did not come here to argue the merits of our past relationships. Sufficient to say that you do not appear to have suffered by them. You are still as beautiful as ever—and no doubt duping some other poor fool, as you once did my brother!'

Ashley's fingers stung across his cheek, almost before he had finished speaking, and she watched in horror as the marks she had made appeared on his dark skin. She waited in silent apprehension for him to retaliate in kind, as he had once done in the past, but apart from lifting a brown-fingered hand to finger his bruised cheek, he took no immediate retribution.

'So,' he said at last. 'Now you have relieved yourself of such pent-up energy, perhaps we can now get to the point of my visit.'

'What point?' Ashley was sullen, as much from a sense of self-recrimination as from anything he had said. She had made a fool of herself, not him, by her childish display of temper, and it was up to her now to prove that she could be as controlled as he was.

'Perhaps if you were to offer me a cup of coffee,' he said, indicating her cup nearby. 'Obviously I have interrupted you. If we were to behave more as—acquaintances than enemies——'

'Oh, for God's sake!' Ashley's nerve snapped again, and she turned away from him abruptly, feeling the hot tears stinging in her eyes. It was no use. She could not be unemotional about this, and she groped for a tissue to wipe away the evidence.

'You are behaving foolishly,' exclaimed Alain's voice behind her, and in spite of her confusion at his sudden nearness, she thought she detected a trace of reluctant remorse in his tone. 'I do not wish to resurrect old hatreds,' he added roughly. 'I only wish to speak with you, Ashley, to offer you my help.'

'Your *help*?' Ashley spun round to face him then, tilting back her head so that she could look into his eyes. He had always been taller than she was, even though she was not a small girl, but barefoot as she was his advantage was greater. She gazed into those enigmatic blue eyes, so startlingly unusual in such an alien countenance, and her lips parted in disbelief. 'You want to help me?' she whispered, moving her head from side to side, and his long silky lashes drooped to narrow the pupils.

'Yes,' he said curtly. 'That was my only intention. But you do not make good intentions easy.'

'You? With *good* intentions?' Ashley's lips quivered. 'I don't believe it.'

Alain's jaw hardened. 'Have a care, Ashley. You have tried my patience once this afternoon. Do not push your luck. I may not be so lenient the second time around.'

Ashley held up her head. 'Then go! I didn't ask you to come here. I—I want nothing from the Gauthiers. Nothing!'

'Nothing?'

'Except perhaps—my son,' she conceded almost inaudibly, and then winced when his hands closed on her shoulders, biting into the soft flesh, bruising the bone.

'Do not say that again,' he commanded harshly. 'I told you this morning. Hussein is not your son. He has never been your son. He has been brought up to believe he is an orphan, that his mother died along with his father——'

'*No!*' Ashley caught her breath, but Alain was merciless.

'Yes,' he declared grimly. 'So far as Hussein is concerned, you do not exist. And you must not exist, is that understood?'

Ashley tried to pull away from him, but he would not let her go, and her fury erupted into passion. 'Why are you doing this, Alain?' she cried, balling her fists and attempting to strike him. 'Why are you telling me these things? Haven't I suffered enough, is that it? Don't you have any pity, any compassion? How do you think I felt, seeing my own son, knowing he didn't recognise me? What more do you want of me, you bastard!'

'You have a viper's tongue, Ashley,' he drawled, but she could tell her insults had annoyed him. 'However, I am prepared to believe that seeing the boy has temporarily unhinged your brain, and therefore I will not re-taliate in kind.'

'How good of you!' Ashley threw back her head as the heavy weight of her hair fell across her forehead. 'Well, let me tell you, I was never more sane in my life, and I don't need your tolerance or your offer of help!'

Alain's expression was grim. 'Nevertheless, you will listen to me.'

'Will I? Will I?' Ashley deliberately taunted him, knowing she was nearing the end of her nervous reserves, desperate for him to go before she broke down com-pletely. 'And how will you make me? By—by fair means—or foul?'

Alain shook her, forcefully, so that her head swayed alarmingly back and forth, the swinging curtain of her hair seeming to make it almost too heavy for her slender neck to support. 'I came to the school to withdraw Hus-sein's name from the register,' he grated savagely. 'I do not know why I brought him with me, except perhaps that he wanted to come. I did not expect to see you. The school is not due to open for two days. How was I to know that one of its teachers——'

Ashley's head lolled back. 'You mean—you *knew*!'

'That you were employed there, yes. Since I brought Hussein to London, I found out.'

Ashley blinked. 'And—and that was why you wanted to withdraw his name?'

'Of course.' Alain looked down at his fingers digging into the fine cotton of her smock, and allowed them to slacken slightly. 'You do not suppose I would permit otherwise?'

Ashley tried to think, but coherent thought was diffi-cult. 'A-and?'

'Your Mr Henley explained that you had resigned,' he replied flatly. 'For the same reason, one would suppose.'

'One would suppose correctly,' said Ashley tautly. 'So?'

'So—Hussein's name remains on the register. At least, until this matter is settled.'

'What matter?'

'The matter of your employment,' said Alain, releasing her abruptly to thrust his hands into the pockets of his dark trousers. And as she gazed at him nonplussed: 'I have a proposition to put to you.'

Ashley's tongue came to circle her lips. 'A proposition?' she echoed, even as her brain refused to take it in. She was still stunned by the knowledge that he had known of her involvement with Brede School before their encounter that morning, and she knew him too well to trust any proposal he might make.

'Won't you sit down now?' he suggested briefly, indicating the couch behind him, but Ashley shook her head.

'Thank you, I prefer to stand,' she retorted coldly, and had the satisfaction of seeing that she had annoyed him once again.

'Very well,' he said at last, moving away from her, and she had a momentary premonition that he was not as controlled as he appeared. Just for a second, when he looked at her, she had glimpsed a curious expression in his eyes, but then the mask fell into place and he was once more his father's eldest son.

'There is a post,' he said, standing before the screened fireplace with his back to her. 'In Cairo. A friend of mine requires a governess for his two daughters. It will be a well-paid position, with every amenity available to someone of your——'

'*No!*' The word burst from Ashley in incensed denial. 'No, I don't want your rotten post! My work is here, in England. If I choose to take a private position, it will be of my choosing, not yours!'

'Do you not wish to work in Egypt, is that it? You would prefer some other place?' Alain still did not turn. 'Perhaps I could make other arrangements——'

'No!' Ashley's response was the same, and now he did turn, slowly, to face her.

'You will not change your mind?' he enquired, his face grim, and she shook her head. 'Very well, then. I will withdraw Hussein from the school.'

'Why? Ashley took an involuntary step towards him,

her bewilderment plain. 'Why? I've resigned—Malcolm told you that. What more do you want?'

'Malcolm?' Alain's dark brows arched interrogatively. 'Who is—Malcolm?'

'Malcolm Henley,' exclaimed Ashley impatiently. 'Mr Henley, the headmaster.'

Alain's mouth tightened. 'It would appear you know him better than I thought,' he said accusingly. 'He is your—friend, perhaps. Your—lover?'

Ashley's face flamed. 'No! That is—Malcolm is a friend, yes.' And then, realising she was stammering like a schoolgirl, she added fiercely: 'It's no business of yours what our relationship is.'

Alain stiffened. 'Then he is your lover. And this is why you do not wish to leave London.'

'No!' Ashley didn't know why she felt the need to defend herself, but she did. 'I simply don't want to leave my home, this apartment; and—and all my friends.'

Alain breathed deeply. 'Then I have no choice.'

'Why not?' Ashley linked her fingers together as an idea occurred to her. 'Are you afraid I'll try to see—to see him? To identify myself to him?'

Alain bent his head. 'The situation is hypothetical. I will not leave him here.'

'Don't you trust me, Alain?' she exclaimed, and he lifted his head to look at her.

'Is there any reason why I should?' he retorted bleakly, and a small gasp of pain escaped her.

'Yes,' she retorted fiercely. 'Yes. I—I've never lied to you——'

'We will not go into that,' he interrupted her harshly. 'Lies, deceptions, call it what you will, I have no time to concern myself with such things. They are over, in the past, and the past is dead.'

'No. No, it's not.' Ashley was indignant. 'You can't say these things to me and expect no retaliation. And why shouldn't I see my son? Even divorced women have such rights.'

'Not in my country,' retorted Alain shortly, raising one

hand to massage the back of his neck, as if he was tense too. 'Ashley, why can you not be reasonable? You need another post. I am offering you one. According to your— friend Henley, you will not find it easy to take up another appointment at this time.'

Ashley faltered. 'What did you say to him? What did you tell him?'

Alain shrugged. 'Only that I was withdrawing Hussein from the school.'

'Nothing else?'

His expression grew remote. 'You think I would discuss my private affairs with a stranger?'

Ashley shook her head. 'Then how did you find out I was leaving?'

Alain frowned. 'It was Henley. He made the point that perhaps I was unhappy that Hussein's form tutor was to be a woman, and went on to explain that you had handed in your resignation. Naturally, I agreed to give the matter further consideration.'

'I see.' Ashley nodded, but now Alain looked wary.

'Why?' he pressed her. Then, with a darkening anger: 'Does Henley know of this matter? You cannot have told him that Hussein is your son!'

He was incensed, and she felt a bitter sense of satisfaction. 'Why not?' she taunted. 'I told you, Malcolm is a friend, as well as my superior.'

'*Diable!*' Alain crossed the floor towards her in two savage strides. 'You are telling me this man is familiar with our private affairs? That you have confided our most personal relationships to him?'

Ashley quivered. 'He only knows that—that Andrew is my son——'

'Only!' Alain swore angrily. '*Nom de Dieu!* The situation gets worse. You had no right to betray such information.'

'Betray?' Ashley gazed up at him, noticing almost inconsequently the erratic flutter of the pulse that marked his jawline. 'Alain, you can't deny me the right to acknowledge my son. Besides,' she moistened her lips, 'how else could I have resigned at the beginning of term? What excuse could I give? Malcolm would have suspected——'

'Malcolm! Malcolm! I begin to grow tired of this man's name,' declared Alain violently, his blue eyes searching her face with angry intensity. 'So—it is over. It is finished. I will take Hussein back to Khadesh!'

'No——'

Ashley's involuntary plea was accompanied by her hand on his arm, gripping the taut muscle she could feel through the expensive cloth of his sleeve. It was more than seven years since she had touched Alain, more than seven years since he had arrived at the hospital in Paddington and taken away the only tangible proof of her brief, but brutal, association with the Gauthier family. But she was appealing to him now, raising herself on her toes to bring her face nearer to his, unconsciously by her actions drawing his attention to the agitated swell of her breasts, outlined against the thin material of her smock.

'Ashley!' he grated, and when he spoke, his voice was deepened by some savage emotion he was trying hard to contain. 'In the name of all the saints, Ashley, get away from me, before I am compelled to deliver the punishment I should have administered years ago!'

'What punishment?' Ashley's lips parted, but she did not move away from him. It was a curious anomaly, but suddenly she sensed that for all his anger and his threats of violence, he was not as indifferent to her as he would like her to believe. Was it possible? she asked herself incredulously. After all these years, was it conceivable that he had some regrets for the pain and misunderstandings of the past? But no! That was not like Alain. He had always been so controlled, so positive, so remote from the weaknesses of the flesh. *Except when he had been in her arms*, a small voice reminded her wickedly, and an insane desire to find out if she was right gripped her. With a fast-beating heart she allowed her other hand to rest against his chest, in the hollow of the vee where the fastening of his waistcoat began, and deliberately spread her fingers against the fine silk of his shirt.

'Ashley!' His free hand caught her tormenting fingers, crushing them within the strength of his as he impaled her with an impassioned glare. 'Do not try your feminine wiles on me! That was over long ago, and you would do well to remember that you are my brother's widow!'

'I haven't forgotten it,' she protested huskily, aware of the convulsive shudder that had passed through him before he captured her fingers in his. 'Perhaps—perhaps it is yourself you have to convince!'

'No!' His jaws were clamped together, and he spoke through his teeth, but Ashley had aroused him, and she was not prepared to lose her advantage.

'He's my son, Alain,' she breathed, moving closer to him, so that the pointed tips of her breasts actually brushed against the hand imprisoning hers. 'Don't take him away again—*please*! I promise I won't tell him who I am. I only want to *see* him again, to look at him, maybe speak with him——'

'It is not possible!'

The words were torn from him, and looking up into his dark face, Ashley knew a moment's fear for what she was provoking. She had loved this man, she remembered painfully, she had cared for him with every fibre of her being. Even after all that had happened, could she be sure she could control her feelings, and use them to defeat him?

Her breath fanned his chin, warm and sweet, mingling with the scent of her body. Her agitation had brought a film of perspiration over her skin, and its odour was musky and sensual. The smock was loose and revealing, something casual, to be worn around the flat, and the baggy pants hinted at the swell of her hips and the long slender length of her legs. She knew Alain was looking at her, absorbing her body's freedom, and after the enveloping garments worn by the women in his own country she must seem the epitome of liberated womanhood.

'This has got to stop!' he ordered vehemently, but his intention to push her away from him was foiled by Ashley slipping her arms around his neck. It brought her close against him, her forehead on a level with his lips, and she looked up at him through her lashes, her green eyes soft and appealing.

'Alain,' she breathed, and his control snapped. His hands at her waist were hard and ungentle, jerking her against him with urgent compulsion. His mouth too was hot and aggressive, searing her lips with a brutal tempestuous possession that had nothing of love in it.

'Is this what you want, Ashley?' he demanded, against her mouth, almost suffocating her with the burning heat of his breath. 'Do you want to be treated the way my father's ancestors treated their women? Without honour or respect?' Yet, in spite of his anger, she sensed the desperation in his voice and the hungry passion beneath his cruel strength.

'Is that what you want, Alain?' she asked, turning his words back on him, as his teeth fastened on the tender lobe of her ear, and he bit it. She winced, but she did not draw away, as she added unevenly: 'Do you enjoy inflicting pain?'

'Yes,' he told her, in a raw anguished tone, and then again: 'No! Damn you, no!' as her hands turned his face to hers, and she put her mouth next to his. His lips parted almost involuntarily, and her mouth opened to accommodate his. She welcomed his intimate invasion, the sensuous brush of passion, that was so much more devastating than brute force. With a little moan of pleasure, that was by no means contrived, she moulded herself against him, and his hands probed beneath the smock to find the smooth skin of her back.

It was strange how time rolled back under the hungry pressure of his lips. Without her being aware of it, her response changed from the controlled reaction to a planned set of circumstances, to an eager and willing consummation of his possession. She pressed herself against him, uncaring when her fingernails raked the hair at the nape of his neck.

'*Ashley!*' Alain's strangled voice came to her as if from a distance, and at first she didn't want to pay any attention to it. But when he dragged his mouth from hers and lifted his head, she was forced to acknowledge that the situation was rapidly slipping from her grasp. With a little shiver she lowered her toes to the floor, and forced herself to look up at him questioningly as he strove for his own sanity. 'Ashley—for God's sake——'

'You wanted to touch me,' she said simply, and his hands dropped abruptly to his sides.

'You are a madness—and a temptation,' he retorted, in a shaken tone. 'Are you wearing anything under—under that outfit?'

'Not much,' she conceded huskily, realising she had little time left to make any headway. 'Do you want to see?'

'*No!*' Alain turned aside from her, combing somewhat unsteady fingers through his thick dark hair. 'I have to go. There—are things I have to do.'

'Will I see you again?' she enquired softly, and he gave her a brooding stare.

'It is unlikely. I intend to return to Khadesh at the end of the week.' He paused. 'I *shall* be taking Hussein with me.'

It was a bitter blow, but not unexpected. Nevertheless, she still had one more card to play, a card which had only just occurred to her.

'And—his education?' she asked. 'What about that?'

'I will make other arrangements,' declared Alain curtly, rapidly recovering his composure. 'That need not concern you——'

'Oh, but it does,' she contradicted him softly. 'You see, I think he might benefit from private tuition.'

'Private tuition?' Alain frowned. 'Well—perhaps.'

'And I can supply it,' inserted Ashley quietly.

'What!' Alain was incredulous at first, and then he gave a harsh laugh. 'You are not serious!'

'Oh, but I am.' Ashley held up her head. 'And unless you want me to create a great deal of unpleasantness, you should agree with me.'

Alain stared at her. 'Are you threatening me, Ashley?'

Ashley's skin prickled at the sudden malevolence of his gaze. Only rarely did Alain assume the arrogant hawklike countenance of his father's forebears, those wild and lawless Arab tribesmen who for centuries had lived like lords in their desert kingdom. But right now he possessed all their savage ruthlessness and hauteur, and she faltered for a moment on the brink of submission.

But then the realisation of what she was fighting for strengthened her will, and facing him bravely she said: 'And if I am?'

Alain speared her with his scorching glare. 'And how do you propose to create this unpleasantness?'

Ashley's lips parted. 'I—I——' she faltered again, and then, as his lips curled contemptuously, she burst out: 'The—the authorities. I could go to the authorities. I could tell them how you intimidated me, how you made me hand my baby over to you——'

'You would not do such a thing!' Alain menaced her, but she held her ground.

'I would. Yes, I would.' She fought free of his mesmerising stare. 'And they'd listen to me, too—you know they would. You could face court proceedings, particularly if I said you threatened me——'

'Be silent!' Alain was furious. 'You must be crazy if you imagine I'll let you blackmail me!'

Ashley backed away from him. 'Not crazy, just desperate,' she spat at him resentfully. 'And don't think that's all. There are other ways.'

'I am sure there are.' Alain's eyes were dark and brooding now, their blueness overlaid by a film of frustration. 'Nevertheless, you are insane if you think I will permit you to teach the boy. If that were so, what point would there be in my taking him away from the school?'

'Private tutoring is different,' Ashley declared, touching her bruised lips with a nervous finger. 'And—and you would be there to—to watch your—investment.'

Alain shook his head. 'And for this—privilege, you will promise—what?'

'Not to tell him who I am.'

'And why should I believe you?'

'Because I don't tell lies,' retorted Ashley forcefully. 'I don't. I never have——'

'Enough of that!' Alain paced the floor in evident impatience. 'And how can I be sure that once you have achieved this objective, you will not demand others?'

'What others?'

'Do not be naïve,' he snapped. 'You think to insinuate your way into his life by one means or another.'

Ashley licked her lips. 'And are you going to let me?'

'My father would never permit you to enter the palace.'

'Your father need not know who I am. He's never seen me.' She paused. 'Only you—and—and Hassan ever——'

'Enough!' rasped Alain again, stopping his pacing to stare at her once more. 'And if I still refuse?'

Ashley shrugged. 'I—I'll get to Andrew, somehow. And I'll tell him everything. Everything!'

'Knowing he would never forgive you for it?' mocked Alain coldly.

'What have I to lose?' she retorted. Then: 'Well? Will you do it?'

Alain's mouth was a thin line. 'I will have to think about it.'

'For how long?'

'I don't know.' He turned away abruptly. 'Give me— time. I need time. Twenty-four hours at least.'

'Very well.' Ashley pulled open the door behind her. 'You know where to find me.'

'Oh, yes,' he said bleakly, 'I do indeed.'

And without another word he walked out the door.

CHAPTER THREE

ASHLEY'S elation lasted only so long as it took for Alain to get in the car that was waiting for him, and drive away. As the long black limousine bearing the coat of arms of Prince Ahmed of Khadesh disappeared round a bend in the road, she realised she had no idea where Alain was staying. He had gone, albeit promising to contact her again in twenty-four hours, but if he did not, if he chose to ignore her demands and leave the country, she had no way of stopping him.

Frustration engulfed her, and she sank down on to the couch with a little sound of helplessness. She had been a fool, a stupid fool, and even now Alain was probably exulting over the simple way he had thwarted her. But she had been so excited at the prospect of seeing her son again, of getting to know him, and of having him get to know her, she had not considered the inevitable flaws in her reasoning. She should have known she could not succeed so easily. She should have suspected something was wrong when Alain did not waste time arguing with her.

Getting up from the couch again, she walked restlessly across the room. What should she do? What could she do? And if Alain chose to walk out on her, how was she ever to see Andrew again? Apart from anything else, she was still employed by the governors of the school, and it would be foolish to resign her position there if she had no other employment.

She pushed her fingers into her hair, holding them there as she acknowledged the hopelessness of her position. If only she had not gone into school that morning, she thought despairingly. If Alain had withdrawn Andrew's name, she might never have known anything about it, and her life would not now be suffering the turmoil she was presently experiencing.

A tap at her door brought her round with a start, and almost tripping over herself she rushed to open it. A small, dumpy little woman, wrapped in a dressing gown and wearing carpet slippers, her hair coiled around a series of rollers, stood on the threshold, and Ashley expelled her breath unsteadily as her neighbour began to speak.

'Did you want me, love?' the little woman asked anxiously. 'I was in the bath, but I thought I heard you shouting, and I came round as quickly as I could.'

'Oh, Mrs Forrest.' Ashley caught her lower lip between her teeth, feeling ashamed that she had disturbed her. 'Er—no. No, I wasn't trying to attract your attention. I—I had a visitor. What you heard was—was probably him going.' She crossed her fingers.

'Ah!' Mrs Forrest nodded. 'That would be it, I suppose.' She smiled, patting her rollered head. 'I must look quite a state.' She chuckled. 'And there was me thinking you'd been attacked!'

Ashley coloured. 'I'm very grateful,' she said, almost glad of the diversion. 'Thank you.'

Mrs Forrest had turned away, but she glanced back now over her shoulder. 'For what, dear?'

Ashley shrugged, a little awkwardly. 'Well—for being there.' She hunched her shoulders, pushing her hands into the pockets of her pants. 'Thanks, anyway.'

'You're welcome.'

Mrs Forrest disappeared back into her flat with a wave of her hand, and with a sigh Ashley closed her door again, leaning back against it with a feeling of intense disillusionment. It had all gone wrong, hopelessly wrong, and her only consolation was the realisation that she had provoked Alain. He had not been able to deny his desire for her body, and although this was small comfort when he *had* been capable of walking away from her, given the same circumstances, she might be able to repeat her success. She squashed the uneasy recollection that she had been as aroused by his lovemaking as he was. It was a sexual response, nothing more. Any woman, kissed by a man as virile and attractive as Alain Gauthier, would find it extremely difficult to keep a cool head in such circumstances, and in her case, the memories of the past kept intruding. Once she had succeeded in exorcising those painful images she would be able to control her own destiny again. She had loved him in those days. She did not love him now. But she would use him, in any way she could, if it meant she could be near her son.

Shaking her head, she moved away from the door. Was she really so determined about this? she asked herself with sudden uncertainty. Why, after all these years, was she even considering such a course of action? The answer was simple. It was as she had always known it would be. So long as her son was unknown to her, so long as she had no image of him in her mind, she could pretend he didn't exist. But now she had seen him, he had smiled at her; and she would move heaven and earth to be near him again.

She was still trying to formulate some plan of action when the telephone rang. Picking up the receiver, she wondered if Alain was ringing to taunt her with her helplessness, but it was Malcolm Henley at the other end of the line.

'Ashley? My dear, I just thought I'd tell you, your resignation will not be necessary.'

Ashley moistened her lips. 'It won't?'

'No.' Malcolm sounded pleased. 'I've just had a telephone call from Gauthier—you know, your brother-in-law?'

'Yes?' Ashley's hand trembled.

'Yes.' Malcolm paused, as if timing his announcement. 'He's asked me to withdraw Hussein's name from the register. He's changed his mind, apparently. He's going to have the boy educated in Murad.'

Ashley drew an unsteady breath. 'I see.'

'Isn't that good news?' Malcolm was obviously disappointed at her response. 'You don't know this, but he actually came to see me this morning, bringing the boy with him. He'd read your name on the——'

'I know.' Ashley was too disturbed to allow him to go through the whole rigmarole of telling her something she already knew.

'You know?' Malcolm sounded bewildered. 'But how?'

'Alain's been here, too,' she replied unwillingly. 'He—well, I encountered them in school this morning, and he came here to offer me a private position, with some family in Egypt.'

'I see.' Malcolm was perturbed. 'So you met the boy. How unfortun——' He broke off abruptly, then added crisply: 'You told Gauthier you couldn't take the job, didn't you?'

Ashley opened her mouth to say yes, then closed it again. She had no intention of discussing her plans with Malcolm, and it might actually be simpler if he thought she was considering a post with some unknown Egyptian family. It would give her a breathing space.

'I—I haven't made up my mind yet,' she said now, and heard Malcolm's impatient intake of breath.

'But if Gauthier is withdrawing—well, there's no need for you to consider another job,' he exclaimed. 'I don't know why he's changed his mind, but he has. I did tell him that you'd resigned, and I thought he seemed satisfied, but now—this!' He hesitated. 'You—well, you didn't say anything which might have influenced him, did you?'

Ashley was indignant. 'Malcolm!'

'It was only a thought. I'm sorry.' He was apologetic. 'But you must admit, it's strange that he should back out—now.'

Ashley moved her shoulders. 'Perhaps he's decided to—employ a private tutor,' she ventured, hardly daring to hope, but Malcolm's diagnosis was not encouraging.

'I think he's decided there are too many temptations for a young boy growing up in this country,' he remarked sourly. 'You should know how strictly they cling to the old traditions. I'm more inclined to believe he'll be sent to one of those military establishments when he's older, where the discipline is more severe.'

Ashley could not prevent the involuntary cry of protest that escaped her then, and as if just realising he was speaking to the boy's mother, Malcolm cursed his reckless tongue. 'Of course, I don't mean that the boy will suffer in any way from it,' he declared hastily. 'I may be entirely wrong.' He sighed. 'In any event, I'm sure his uncle will keep a careful eye upon him.'

'I'm sure he will.' Ashley's tone was taut with suppressed emotion.

'So—I'll see you tomorrow, shall I?' Malcolm suggested uncomfortably. 'Nine o'clock, as usual.'

'I don't know.' Ashley was confused, and Malcolm made a sound of impatience.

'Oh, come along, Ashley! It's not the end of the world, you know. I realise seeing the boy must have been a traumatic experience for you, but it's over now. He's going back to Murad, and there's no earthly reason why you shouldn't continue in your position here.'

Ashley could feel the tears pricking at her eyes again, and sniffed them back. 'I—I don't know what I shall do, Malcolm,' she said, which was the truth. 'Right now, I—I'm not feeling very well. I—I may take tomorrow off. It's not necessary for me to be there, is it? School doesn't really begin until the next day.'

'No. No, but you know how hectic everything is at the start of the new year. Boys arriving from all over the place, beds to make and allocate, timetables to be explained——'

'It's not really my job, is it, Malcolm?' Ashley reminded him tautly, feeling mean, but needing the time to think. 'I'll do what I can.'

'I'm sure you will, my dear.'

Malcolm's words were intended to be conciliatory, but Ashley couldn't forget the insensitivity he had just displayed. He had said he cared about her, but all he really cared about was the school, and the significance of her meeting with Andrew was lost on him. He thought she should dismiss the fact that she had just met her son for the first time, and carry on as if nothing untoward had happened. He expected her to go into the school tomorrow and help organise the domestic staff while he concerned himself with names and addresses. *Addresses!*

Her hand shook so much she could hardly grip the receiver, but she managed to hold on. 'By the way,' she said, as he was about to ring off, 'did you have an address for—for the Gauthiers?'

There was silence for a moment, then Malcolm said rather doubtfully: 'Yes. Why?'

Ashley took a deep breath. 'Alain—he forgot to give me the address to write to, about—about this job I mentioned. Whether I decide to take it or not, I've got to let him know, but——'

'Oh, I see.' Malcolm sounded relieved, and she heard him riffling through the papers on his desk. 'Yes. Yes, here it is. I thought you'd have known it. It's the Askar Palace in Khadesh.'

Ashley's momentary excitement dispersed. 'No,' she exclaimed, 'I—I meant in England. Wh-where is he staying?'

Malcolm checked again. 'That's the only address I have. Besides, as he's flying back to Murad tomorrow, I hardly see——'

'*Tomorrow!*' Ashley's hand flew over the mouthpiece of the telephone to prevent Malcolm from overhearing her horrified exclamation. Then: 'Yes. Yes, you're right. I—I'll contact him there.'

'That's the best idea,' Malcolm approved. 'And—Ashley?'

'Yes?'

'Don't do anything you might afterwards—*regret.*'

He rang off before she could ask him what he meant, but it made her see he was not indifferent to her state of mind. He knew she was distraite, and he was trying to tell her not to do anything foolish.

Pacing the flat later, she wondered whether he was not right, after all. She was considering action which, by any standards, could be regarded as reckless. She could conceivably hurt herself more than she was likely to hurt Alain, with Andrew the innocent pawn in the middle. But then she remembered her son's smiling face, and knew that whatever happened she had to make the attempt.

But how? How? If Alain was planning to leave the following day, he could have no intention of agreeing to her suggestion. He had only agreed to think it over to placate her. His determination to remove the boy from temptation had not faltered.

Straddling a chair by the window, she draped her arm along its back and rested her chin on her wrist. Where was he likely to be staying in London? Not the apartment. She shivered. He had given that up after—well, when she married Hassan. And if the Gauthier organisation had any other property, she was not aware of its whereabouts. Which only left hotels . . .

Getting up, she rescued the commercial edition of the telephone directory, and turned to the relevant section. There were dozens of hotels in and around the London area, but she knew Alain would choose somewhere exclusive, and quiet. Running her finger down the list, she jotted the numbers of half a dozen of the more elegant establishments on to a pad, then picked up the telephone receiver.

Half an hour later she was no further forward. Even when she claimed kinship with the family, none of the receptionists would admit that Prince Alain was staying at their hotel, and while she suspected they might not tell her even if he was, the suspicion was growing that he was staying elsewhere. But where? With relatives? With friends? Or in some other apartment, high above Regent's Park, with a magnificent view over the city?

Sighing, she got up from the couch again and trudged into her bedroom. Her passport was in the drawer of the cabinet beside her bed, and pulling it out, she assured herself of its validity. The last entry in it had been stamped when she went to Paris in the spring, one of the staff accompanying a school party of a dozen older boys. It had been a successful trip and the boys had enjoyed it. And if she had felt a pang at the French capital's association with Alain, and subsequently with her son, she had succeeded in keeping it at bay . . .

Closing the passport again, she tapped it on her palm. She knew, without looking, that she needed no special inoculations before visiting Murad. Like Egypt, it only demanded smallpox and cholera certificates and an injection against yellow fever, if she was coming from an infected area, and unlike Egypt, a visa was not necessary. If she could get on the flight, she could leave for Murad tomorrow, too, with only currency providing any difficulties. It might even be the same flight that Alain and Andrew were taking . . .

With a nervous gesture she dropped the passport back into the drawer and closed it quickly. What was she thinking of? She was still obliged to honour her contract with Brede. How could she consider flying off to the Middle East, without positive proof that Alain would even acknowledge her, let alone employ her?

Nibbling at her thumb, she went back into the living room, unable to remain in one place for any length of time. What time was it? she asked herself unsteadily, and discovering it was after five o'clock, she determinedly marched into the kitchen to prepare herself some food.

But even a plate of soup defeated her, and after swallowing several mouthfuls, she was on her feet again. If only she could get in touch with Alain, she thought bitterly. If only she had asked him where he was staying before all this blew up.

By bedtime, she had forced herself to the realisation that unless Alain contacted her, there was nothing she could do. Once again the Gauthiers had had the last word, and the tears she had been stifling all day soaked her pillow. Oh, Alain, she breathed, at the last, how could you do this to me? And she had no satisfactory explanation for the pain that tore her apart.

In the morning, things looked marginally better. With an autumn sun streaming through her kitchen windows, Ashley felt almost resigned as she prepared her toast and coffee, and carrying the morning newspaper to the dining room table she propped it against the marmalade pot as she buttered her toast.

There were the usual headlines—another strike in the Midlands, an escape from custody of a wanted criminal, more unpopular governmental decisions—and after skipping through these, Ashley turned to the gossip columns. It was a relief to read about someone else's problems, she thought, sympathising with the fight an actress was having in establishing her rights as a famous actor's common-law wife. Without the security of a wedding ring, a woman had few privileges, she acknowledged flatly, and even with one, a man always had the ascendancy.

Her lips tightened. It wasn't fair, she fretted, her eyes registering a mute protest. Andrew was her son! Was he to grow to manhood without even speaking a word to the woman who had borne him in her body for nine whole months?

The telephone bell interrupted her melancholy abstraction, and it rang several times before she stirred herself to go and answer it. She didn't feel like talking to anybody right now, and she lifted the receiver with dour reluctance.

'Yes?'

'Ashley?'

Her knees gave out on her, and she sank down weakly on to the couch. 'Al-Alain?'

'You did not expect me to ring?'

'No—yes. I mean——' Ashley struggled to shake off her apathy. 'Why are you calling? To let me know you're leaving today? I know that already—Malcolm told me. He said you'd definitely withdrawn Andrew's name from the register, and as you conveniently forgot to give me your address, I suppose you're ringing to flaunt your advantage——'

'Do you want to hear what I have to say, or do you not?' Alain interposed curtly, cutting into her babbling tirade. 'I told you I would consider your proposition, and I have. Where I am staying in London does not seem of great relevance.'

Ashley's jaw shook. 'Well, all right. What have you decided? That I won't do? That I'm not suitable? That you couldn't possibly employ a woman to teach the boy, and that in any case your father would never agree to it?'

'Will you stop trying to pre-empt me?' Alain's voice betrayed his irritation now. 'In the name of Allah, you seem to be doing your best to persuade me that you are not suitable!'

Ashley faltered, 'What do you mean?'

'What do you think I mean?'

Ashley's palms were moist. 'You can't mean—you don't mean——' Her voice shook. 'Oh, Alain! You wouldn't tease me, would you?'

'No,' he said flatly, 'I would not tease you. And you have yet to decide whether what I have to say is acceptable to you.'

Ashley swallowed convulsively. 'Go on.'

Alain hesitated, then he said briefly: 'Your initial contract will be made for a probationary period of a month. If, at the end of that time, the arrangement has proved—unsatisfactory—to either party, it can be terminated forthwith.'

Ashley breathed out quickly: 'All right.'

'This is to be a business arrangement only,' Alain continued. 'With certain—clauses inserted, relevant to the situation.'

Ashley quivered. 'What clauses?'

Alain paused. 'A sworn undertaking from you that you will not, at any time, and to anybody, divulge your relationship to Hussein.'

Ashley's stomach churned. 'Is that all?'

'No. In addition, I shall want your written agreement that you handed over Hussein independently, and of your own free will, and that you have no intention of asserting your rights as his mother in the future.'

'No!' Ashley's voice broke on the word. 'Alain, you're unreasonable. You can't make me sign something like that.'

'Then you must do what you can to gain your own ends,' he declared roughly. 'There is nothing more to be said.'

'*Wait!*' Ashley could not let him go like that. 'Alain, give me a few moments, at least. Let me think!"

'I do not have much time, Ashley. We leave for the airport in less than half an hour.'

'You're leaving?' she gasped, in consternation.

'You said you knew,' he reminded her.

'Well, yes, but——' Ashley sought for words. 'I thought—now——'

'If you decide to accept the position, you will follow us, after you have completed your term of notice,' he replied smoothly. 'It is better this way. It will enable me to prepare the ground, as you might say. And give you time to resign yourself to the situation.'

Ashley shook her head. 'You—you're inhuman!'

'Merely practical,' he amended dryly. 'Well? Have you reached a decision?'

Ashley tipped back her head, as if her neck ached. It was too much. How could she sign away her child's birthright? But if she did not, she might never see him again. Was the one any worse than the other?

'And—and who will be his guardian?' she asked huskily. 'Who—who has custody of him?'

'Who has always had custody of him?' retorted Alain punishingly. 'Myself—Alain Gauthier.'

Ashley expelled her breath weakly. 'Very well.'

'You'll do it?' Alain sounded incredulous.

'Why not?' Ashley felt suddenly very weary. 'You hold all the cards, Alain. And I haven't the strength to fight you.'

'You realise this arrangement can only last for two years—three at the most?' he exhorted. 'Hussein will go to boarding school eventually. When he is older—and wiser.'

Ashley sighed. 'What do you want me to do?'

There was silence for a moment, then Alain spoke again, giving her details of his arrangements. 'The contract will be drawn up by a firm of London solicitors who handle the Gauthier business here in England,' he declared brusquely. 'They will contact you, when it is ready for your signature, and they will also arrange your travel documents, tickets, and so on. I assume you have a current passport, and that you are not suffering from any transmittable disease.'

'No.' Ashley's voice was scarcely audible. 'Is that all?'

Alain made a sound of impatience. 'Are you sure you want to go through with this?'

'Do you care?' There was a note of indifference in Ashley's voice now.

'You may regret it,' he said harshly. 'The boy is your son.'

Ashley's mouth twisted. 'So much for motherly love,' she choked bitterly, and put down the receiver before she could change her mind.

CHAPTER FOUR

THERE was blue sea below the aircraft again now, as there had been during the flight across the Mediterranean. But now it was the translucent waters of the Arabian Sea, as the plane began to lose height, preparing to make its approach to the airport just outside Khadesh. Ashley's stomach was churning so badly, she could hardly sit still. She felt alternately sick and exhilarated, apprehensive of her reception by Alain's family, yet excited at the prospect of being with Andrew. *Hussein,* she corrected herself fiercely, repeating his Arab name under her breath. She must never forget, she was merely his governess, and as such, not entitled to address him by any other than his given name.

It was almost three weeks since that fateful morning when Alain had brought the boy to school. Three weeks, during which time she had broken the ties with her old life, in spite of opposition from all sides. Malcolm had not approved, but that had not been entirely unexpected. He was upset at losing a valued member of his staff, and, she had to admit it, distressed, too, on a more personal level. Perhaps he did care about her in his own way, she acknowledged, but he had been a bachelor for so long, he had forgotten how to show his true feelings. She dismissed the thought that so far as she knew, Alain was a bachelor, too. They had lived a different kind of life, and Malcolm really believed she would regret putting her emotions before commonsense. She couldn't help wondering how he would have reacted if she had confided the whole story to him, and squashed the unwilling conclusion that that was why she had kept the details of her employment to herself.

What had disturbed her most was Mrs Armstrong's reaction to her plans. She had spent last weekend with the family, needing their support and reassurance at this time, but ultimately gaining neither.

'You'll regret it, Ashley!' Mrs Armstrong exclaimed, after the girl had confessed that Alain had his own methods of ensuring her silence. 'My dear child, you're just creating trouble for yourself later on. Don't you see? This man must realise what will happen when you're in contact with the boy every day. You'll become attached to him, you'll find yourself caring for him; and when the time comes for you to leave, you're going to be torn to pieces!'

Ashley had drawn her knees up then, sitting on the floor in front of the Armstrongs' cheerful log fire, and endeavoured to defend the decision she had taken. 'Isn't it better that I spend some time with him now?' she protested. 'He doesn't know me. He might never know me any other way. Isn't it conceivable that even this small share of his affections is better than nothing?'

'Ashley may have a point,' Lucy had defended, secure now in her own love for a neighbouring farmer, and their proposed marriage in the spring. 'After all, Alain's not going to let her see the boy any other way.'

'She should have fought for him through the courts,' declared Mrs Armstrong firmly. 'That's what they're for.'

'She's right, lass,' Mr Armstrong had supported his wife. 'Legal—that's the only way to do it.'

'But we've all seen how legalities have been over-thrown!' Ashley exclaimed. 'My son is a citizen of Murad. His father—his *grand*father is a powerful man in political circles. Do you think I would stand any chance against that kind of influence?'

'You should,' Mrs Armstrong protested, but Ashley only shook her head.

'Even if I won the case, there's not a chance in a million that they'd let me keep him,' she sighed. 'He lives in Khadesh. What earthly use are our laws, when Murad can overturn them?'

They all agreed that she had a point, nevertheless she knew that they thought she had signed away her child's birthright. And so she had, she thought bitterly. And for what? A month of her son's time—for she had few doubts that she would be found unsuitable, and dismissed at the end of four weeks. But that was something she had told no one, not even the Armstrongs.

Her communication with the Gauthiers had been confined to the medium of their solicitors, Messrs. Stoneham and Laurence, of Grays Inn. Ray Stoneham, grandson of the founder of the firm, and son of the present partner, dealt with her case, and although he might have found the circumstances unusual, his attentions were not entirely altruistic. He evidently found Ashley an intriguing mixture of sophistication and naïveté, and towards the end of their association had invited her to lunch with him. Ashley had politely declined, pleading a previous engagement, but it had been somewhat reassuring to find herself in that position, after years of keeping the opposite sex at bay.

From the air, Murad had a bare, uninhabited appearance. Miles and miles of desert stretched back to the distant hills, and such townships as there were seemed small and remote. The refinery at Zarif, the core of the nation's economy, was along the coast from Khadesh, and Ashley had read that eighty per cent of the population made their home in the capital. The rest eked out a nomadic living in the desert, caring for their sheep and goats, as they had done for centuries, and the fierce wild tribesmen had long been tamed.

The airport, perhaps not surprisingly, was modern and effective, and Ashley, trying to keep her mind from more personal matters, decided that it needed to be. A country's economy depended on the efficiency of its transport, and businessmen and Arab sheiks alike demanded a standard of practice that had to be maintained.

The flight had taken more than seven hours, but Ashley did not feel tired. As she checked her passport and collected her luggage, she was too keyed up to consider her body's weariness, and shunning the attentions of an Arab porter, she carried her own suitcases through to the reception hall.

It was early evening in Murad, and the crimson rays of the setting sun bathed the airport buildings in a roseate glow. Ashley seemed to be the only woman travelling alone, and as she paused in the air-conditioned lounge and looked about her, she realised how conspicuous she was. Perhaps she should have employed the porter after all, she reflected doubtfully. She did not like the curious glances being sent in her direction, or the amused specu- lation she was attracting.

She considered stepping outside the building, but the unexpected coolness of the air discouraged her, and besides, she felt safer, if only marginally, within these walls. She was beginning to realise she should have worn something less revealing than the plain black corded pants suit, but in the chill of an English autumn it had seemed the ideal choice, and the fact that it was black should have made her inconspicuous. She had not given much thought to the fact that black was a perfect foil for her honey-blonde hair, secured now in a neat coil at the nape of her neck, or considered that in a country where women wore shapeless black robes to conceal their shape from masculine eyes, the short jacket and form-fitting pants drew attention to the very attributes she had hoped to disguise. She wished desperately that Alain had been there to meet her. For all her antipathy towards the man himself, she knew he would not have permitted her to stand here at the mercy of these prying eyes, and she looked about her anxiously, wondering if there had been some hold-up in communications. How terrible it would be, she thought, if the Gauthiers had not received details of her travel arrangements. Was it possible for a woman to hire a taxi here, and make her own way to the Askar Palace?

There was a sudden stir outside the building as a low black limousine drew up at the row of sliding glass panels. Someone of importance was evidently arriving, and Ashley took a step forward, straining to see if it was Alain.

But the young man in flowing white robes who stepped from the limousine was not her adversary, and Ashley's shoulders sagged. Her arrival had been evidently overlooked, or else she was expected to make her own way to the palace, and she bent to pick up her cases again, as the newly-arrived entourage swept into the lounge.

'Miss Conway? It is Miss Conway, is it not?'

Ashley straightened in some confusion at the use of the name she had agreed to assume for obvious reasons, her suitcases tugging from her wrists, her lips parting in sudden bewilderment. The young man she had seen arrive had halted in front of her, and it was he who was addressing her, a polite smile tilting the corners of his mouth.

'I—why, yes, I'm—Miss Conway,' she admitted uncertainly, then started as the young man issued a stream of instructions and her suitcases were almost wrenched from her hands.

'I must apologise for not being here to greet you, Miss Conway,' he added, his dark eyes missing no aspect of her appearance, she was sure. 'But, as sometimes happens in your country, there was a snarl-up of traffic, and we were unavoidably delayed.'

'You've come to meet me?' Ashley could hardly believe it. So much ceremony!

'But of course.' The young man bowed, and she noticed the deference of the eyes that watched their little tableau now. 'I am Tariq Anwar, youngest son of my father, the Prince Ahmed, and uncle to your charge, Prince Hussein.'

'I see.' Ashley expelled her breath rather unevenly. She remembered now. Alain and Hassan had had a younger brother, but seven years ago he had been little more than a schoolboy. And he had called her son *Prince* Hussein. This was something she had not even considered.

'You will come with me?' Tariq gestured towards the limousine waiting outside, where her cases had already been stowed. 'My father is waiting to speak with you, and tomorrow you will meet your new charge.'

Ashley's mouth was dry as she accompanied Tariq outside, and climbed into the back of the spacious limousine. Two Arab servants, guards, she supposed, climbed into the back with them, and seated themselves on pull-down seats in front of them. Like Tariq, they also wore the flowing djellaba, and for the first time she wondered whether her son would be dressed in similar clothes. Tariq seated himself beside her on the wide leather rear seat, then with a snap of his fingers they set away, driving smoothly out of the airport complex.

The airport itself was situated on the coastal strip, and as they drove along the wide tarmacked road that led to Khadesh, Ashley could see the surf-edged waters of the ocean creaming along a rocky shoreline. The sea was tinged with the dying rays of the sun, and with the silent depths of the water on one hand, and rolling sand dunes on the other, she knew a momentary fear of what lay ahead of her. She was on Alain's territory now. There was no turning back. And with evidence of the esteem in which his family was held in this country all around her, she knew herself the alien and the interloper.

'I trust you had a good flight.' Tariq was speaking to her now, and Ashley forced herself to concentrate on what he was saying.

'Oh, yes, thank you,' she assured him politely. 'The only turbulence was as we were coming in to land.'

Tariq nodded. 'There is often a wind off the ocean,' he affirmed. 'You may find you are glad of it. It blows as a gentle breeze at Kom Shar, and tempers the atmosphere.' He grimaced. 'It is not like the hot wild wind that blows off the desert. *Sirocco*? You have heard of it, perhaps? It is sometimes called *khamsin*.'

Ashley inclined her head. 'I have heard of it, yes.'

'It has been known to drive people to distraction,' Tariq remarked carelessly. 'But not you, I am sure, Miss Conway.'

'I hope not.' Ashley didn't quite know how to answer him. It was ridiculous, but all she could keep thinking was that this young man was her brother-in-law, and that the man he was taking her to meet was the father of the man she had married. It was incredible—and not a little frightening.

'I think you must be something special,' Tariq continued, much to her embarrassment. 'When my brother, Prince Alain, went to England, it was with the intention of establishing our nephew at a school in London.' He paused. 'You can imagine our astonishment when he returned home with the news that he had changed his mind, and that he had contracted to employ an English governess for the boy.'

Ashley shifted a little uncomfortably. 'I suppose it was quite a—surprise,' she conceded.

Tariq regarded her curiously. 'You do not object to leaving London? The prospect of working in a country where women have but a secondary role does not alarm you?'

'No.' Ashley shook her head. 'Why should it? I—I shall only be working here, after all.'

'This is true,' Tariq acknowledged her reply. 'But no doubt my stepmother, the Princess Hélène, will welcome your presence in the palace. My father's second wife is a Frenchwoman,' he explained, and Ashley's nails dug into her palms as she realised he was referring to Alain's mother.

Darkness was falling as they reached the outskirts of Khadesh, and Ashley stared through the windows of the limousine as they ran through the poorer district of the city. There was still poverty, in spite of the country's reserves of wealth, but efforts were being made to rehouse the inhabitants of these crowded back streets. Here and there were new buildings, residential as well as commercial, with the palm-fringed walls of a modern hospital facing the ruins of a demolition site.

Yet, in spite of this evidence of contemporary architecture, the main streets of the city were lined with much older buildings. The tall spires of the minarets that marked the city's mosques towered above stately houses and museums, with shops and stores set behind avenues of trees, and close by shady parks. Even in the artificial light that streamed from its floodlit buildings, Ashley could see the city was quite beautiful, and totally different from what she had expected. In truth, she didn't quite know what she had expected, but nothing like the grace and symmetry that marked this charming propitiation to Islam.

'This is Mahel al Mansur,' Tariq advised, leaning past her to point out the university buildings. His nearness was not unpleasant, the sweet odour of some perfume that scented his clothes drifting to her nostrils as he moved, but when he turned his head and looked at her, she was slightly alarmed by the liquid softness of his gaze. He was obviously more aware of her than she was of him, and it was not a situation she had any intention of promoting. In consequence she drew back from him perceptibly, adopting a cool indifference, and to her relief he relaxed in his seat once more.

'You are a very attractive woman, Miss Conway,' he remarked unexpectedly, obviously in no way inhibited by the presence of an audience. 'You must forgive me if I find the combination of gold silk and pure alabaster fascinating.' He touched her cheek with a careless finger. 'Your skin is quite exquisite.'

Ashley flinched from his familiar touch, shrinking back into her corner with scarcely concealed dismay. Evidently the young Prince Tariq considered himself equally fascinating, and no doubt regarded a comparatively impoverished English governess as fair play.

When she made no response to his overtures, Tariq's dark brows arched in interrogation. 'Are you not pleased that I find your appearance appealing, Miss Conway?' he suggested. 'I assure you, I am not without discrimination. I have known some of the most beautiful women in the world.'

Ashley half smiled. She supposed that were she a raw governess, meeting one of the Gauthier brothers for the first time, she might be flattered by his attentions. As it was, his almost arrogant approach seemed somehow immature, and compared to Alain's hard features, his face was almost effeminate.

'How old are you, Prince Tariq?' she asked, and was rewarded by an angry glare.

'Old enough,' he retorted, fixing the servants in front of them with a baleful eye, and Ashley turned to the window again, hoping she had not made another enemy.

The squares and formal gardens of the city had given way to suburbs of residential villas with wrought iron gates and screened terraces. Cultivated greenery had a lushness that hinted at the fertility of the soil once the dry earth was irrigated. Palm trees, those most ubiquitous of plants, flourished in great profusion, between luscious flame trees and exotic oleander. The smells of the city were overlaid with the perfumes of the flowers, and it was all new and alien, and disturbingly unfamiliar.

Gradually the houses became more thinly spread, and at last they arrived at sturdy wooden gates set in a high stone wall. Unlike the houses they had passed, the Askar Palace was not visible from the road, and after a white-turbanned servant had flung the gates wide, they drove for some distance between heavily foliaged gardens. The scent of cedar and juniper, of mimosa and eucalyptus, was a potent stimulant, and by the time they passed beneath a stone archway which gave access to a paved courtyard, Ashley's senses were spinning.

It was difficult to assess the size of the house at night, even though the entrance was floodlit. A series of arches seemed to curve away on either side, while ahead of them, one larger than the others gave on to an inner patio. There was the sound of falling water from half a dozen fountains set about the courtyard, and the breeze Tariq had spoken of fanned Ashley's hot cheeks as she descended from the car.

One of the servants had helped her alight, and Tariq walked round the vehicle to join her, flinging one end of his flowing robe over his shoulder. 'Please come with me,' he said, with none of the tolerant good humour he had shown at their meeting, and Ashley, still bemused by the

swarm of white-robed servants who had appeared to
attend to her luggage, could only nod and follow in his
wake.

Lamps swung from every pillar as they traversed the
inner court and entered the palace through arched doors,
that opened almost miraculously at their approach. It
was only as Ashley looked back and saw the servants
bowing behind them that she realised their sole purpose
was to guard the entrance, and she had her first experience of feeling herself a prisoner without bars.

The inner corridor of the palace was also illuminated
by lamps, set in intricately-carved sconces at intervals
along the white marble walls. Adorning the walls were
exquisitely worked scrolls and tapestries, depicting the
history of the area, and ancient weapons in copper and
brass, preserved for future generations. Her heels echoed
loudly in the vaulted hall, but Tariq's sandalled feet scarcely made a sound, and only the swish of his garments
disturbed the cloistered stillness.

It was full dark by this time, and beyond the carved
shutters, narrow windows looked out on to the perfumed
garden. Only occasionally did she glimpse another
human being, guards most likely, patrolling the grounds,
and as her initial bemusement fled, she was left with the
uneasy awareness of where Tariq was taking her. To see
his father, he had said, and her nerves tightened at the
prospect of meeting Prince Ahmed.

Tariq halted before heavy doors, guarded once again
by servants, and this time they were not swung open at
his appearance. The guards came to attention when he
reached the doors, but it was he, and not they, who
knocked for admittance. As his knuckles struck the
panels, he looked at Ashley once more, examining her
face closely, as if seeking some evidence of apprehension.
It took all her powers of self-discipline to sustain that half
resentful appraisal, and presently Tariq was diverted by
the summons from within.

The double doors were opened, and a turbanned man,
with a short beard and moustache, bade them enter. Al-

though his baggy pants and short smock, secured by a
sash, were different from the robes she was beginning to
get used to, Ashley sensed this was not Prince Ahmed. He
would hardly open his own doors, for one thing, she
decided half cynically, and for all his air of authority, the
man bowed his head to her companion.

'Your father is waiting, Prince Tariq,' he informed the
younger man politely, scarcely registering Ashley's presence. 'You are late. The flight was delayed, perhaps.'
Now he flicked a vaguely hostile glance in her direction.
'Come, Prince Ahmed is in the salon.'

'The traffic was heavy,' Tariq conceded, as they
crossed a wide mosaic-tiled floor, and Ashley's relief at
being absolved of blame for their delay was overtaken by
awe at her surroundings. They were in a high-ceilinged
reception room, an enormous apartment, empty now, but
set about with cushioned seats and low tables. There were
flowers everywhere, huge bowls and vases, spilling their
petals on to carved marble plinths, filling the air with
their sweetness. The walls consisted of panels of glazed
tiles, set into the marble, inscribed with Arabic lettering,
and from the centre of the ceiling hung a silver candela-
brum, spreading the light from countless branches.

Beyond the reception room was the salon, entered by
more doors, this time framed in brass, and inlaid with
gold and silver. Ashley had never seen such wealth or
beauty, and her bewilderment helped to keep her fears at
bay. Her eyes were raised to the ceiling as she crossed the
salon's threshold, but they hastily focussed on the room's
occupants when Tariq made his obeisance.

Across a delicately-woven Turkish carpet, two men
awaited their arrival. One, the older man, was seated on
cushions, his robes folded about him. He wore a *haik*,
secured in place by a plaited rope, and the eyes set in a
brown, weathered countenance were sharp and intelligent. Gnarled fingers plucked a handful of grapes from a
bowl at his elbow, and he ate them reflectively as he
studied their approach. He acknowledged his son with
cool consideration, but it was Ashley who held his gaze,

whose appearance aroused most interest.

For her part, Ashley scarcely noticed the older man after a compulsory glance. Her attention was riveted by the man beside Prince Ahmed, and she had to steel herself absolutely to meet his objective stare. Alain stood to one side of his father, and much to her surprise, was not wearing Arab attire. However, his wide-sleeved shirt and black velvet pants, thrust into knee-length leather boots, were not entirely European either, and above the open neck of his shirt Ashley could see the dark shadow of his body hair. He looked powerful, and alien, and remote: and Ashley's determination faltered in the face of his.

'Miss Conway, Father,' Tariq announced formally, and Ashley, dragging her eyes from Alain, wondered rather hysterically whether she was expected to make some obeisance. But she stood her ground, and after a minute's silent consideration Prince Ahmed held out his hand, gesturing her to take a seat.

Ashley sank down on to a pile of cushions, glad, for the first time since her arrival, that she was wearing trousers. At least she did not have to worry about wrapping her skirts around her legs, and she was able to retain a certain degree of modesty.

'You may go, Tariq,' his father said then, clearly disconcerting the younger man, who had obviously expected to remain. 'Alain!' He glanced up at his older son. 'You may leave us also. I wish to speak privately with our new employee.'

'As you wish, Father.'

Alain seemed to accept Prince Ahmed's command without rancour. With a faintly mocking expression marring his lean features, he compelled his brother to walk ahead of him out of the room, and Tariq's indignant features suffused with indignant colour. The man who had let them in did not leave them however. Instead, he stationed himself with his back to the now closed doors, and Ashley was left with the disturbing feeling of being in the presence of an inquisitor.

'Some grapes?'

Prince Ahmed proffered the bowl, but Ashley shook her head. 'Thank you, no,' she refused politely, and he shrugged rather indifferently as he replaced the dish.

'So,' he said, his dark eyes narrowed and intent. 'My son tells me you are a qualified teacher.'

'Yes—er——' Ashley didn't know quite how to address him, and the man who was her son's grandfather inclined his head.

'You may call me Prince Ahmed,' he advised her smoothly. 'And when we are alone together, as now, I shall call you Miss Gilbert.'

Ashley's lips parted. 'My—name——'

'Your name is Ashley Gilbert,' he informed her brusquely. 'Or more precisely Ashley Gauthier. Oh, yes,' this as she gazed at him aghast, 'my son told me who you were. He was obliged to do so. He knew there was no other way I would permit some strange Englishwoman to teach my grandson.'

CHAPTER FIVE

ASHLEY's apartments were in the women's section of the palace. The *seraglio*, she supposed it was called, or more descriptively, the *harem*, although these days there were only two wives to occupy these quarters. Nevertheless, the very fact of their existence filled Ashley with a sense of indignation out of all proportion to their importance, and she bitterly resented being treated as little more than a concubine. Alain's father had made it clear that he regarded a woman with brains to be of rather less standing than one without, and his stubborn resistance to any kind of emancipation for the women of his house was both arrogant and infuriating.

But then he was an arrogant and infuriating man, Ashley acknowledged angrily; their interview had proved that. The initial impact she had felt at learning that he, as well as Alain, knew of her real identity had soon been displaced by a sense of outrage at the insulting things he said to her. She was here, he declared, because Alain had taken seriously her threats of reprisals against the family. He had smiled at this point, but there had been no humour in his face. He, he said, would not have succumbed to such contrived menaces, and he would have found some other method to deal with her hysteria.

'We all know why you married my son,' he said, steepling his fingers and regarding her across them. 'As soon as you became aware of his identity, you conceived your plan to ensnare him, and when Alain proved too elusive you were prepared to settle for Hassan.'

Ashley had been struck dumb by the unfairness of this charge, and taking her silence as acquiescence, Prince Ahmed had continued: 'My son died, Miss Gilbert, in what can only be described as suspicious circumstances. Had it not been for the fact that you proved to be carrying his son, I might well have felt incapable of controlling my desire to take revenge.'

Ashley had scrambled to her feet then, her chest heaving as she struggled to contain her own indignation. 'Your son died by his own hand, *monsieur*!' she declared, ignoring his customary title. 'And so far as my reasons for marrying Hassan are concerned, if I had wanted money—security—call it what you will, I never received a penny!'

Alain's father looked up at her with dislike. 'I have said you may call me Prince Ahmed, Miss Gilbert,' he reminded her. 'Insolence will not be tolerated, whatever the provocation.'

'Won't it? Won't it?' Ashley was too incensed then to care exactly what she was saying. 'And how am I supposed to cope with your insolence, *Prince* Ahmed? First you accuse me of running after your sons, and then you dare to suggest that I might have played some part in Hassan's death! I am not a gold-digger, *Prince* Ahmed. Nor am I a murderess! And if it is your intention to make things so unpleasant for me here that I will wish to resign, then you will have to find some other method of persuasion!'

She had been dismissed then, without further ado. Prince Ahmed had bade the man, Muhammed, to escort her to her apartments, and had made his obeisance to her without even getting up from the cushions. Ashley had sensed Muhammed's disapproval all the way to the women's quarters, and he had left her there, with a dark-skinned servant girl he addressed as Nuzab, with evident satisfaction.

Ashley had to admit that the rooms she had been allocated were spacious and very comfortable. She had been given a suite comprising reception room, salon, bedroom and bathroom, all opening on to an inner court, where a blue-tiled pool invited her participation. The apartment was really too big for someone with the humble status of a governess, but Ashley doubted there were any rooms in the palace that did not possess a natural beauty. The architecture was so typically Moorish in design, with an economy of detail that was simple yet symmetrical. It was made for space and coolness in the heat of the day, and at night, as now, bronze lamps cast their own shadows over jewel-coloured tapestries and soft Bokhara rugs. There were wild silk curtains at the windows, moving sinuously in the draught, and again more bowls of flowers to spread their fragrance. In other circumstances, she could not but have been enchanted by her surroundings, but the recollection of why she was there swept over her in an unrelenting wave.

'You—take bath, *mademoiselle?*' Nuzab questioned at her elbow, and Ashley thrust her depressing thoughts aside and smiled at the Arab girl. Small and delicately formed, Nuzab was an exquisite example of dark-skinned beauty, and her evident desire to please was a salve to Ashley's raw nerves.

'You speak English?' she exclaimed, with some relief, realising as she did so that she had taken it for granted that her son would do likewise, and Nuzab offered a tentative denial.

'Princess Hélène—she teach me a little English, a little French,' she demurred diffidently. 'But Nuzab most happy to try and serve English lady.'

Ashley expelled her breath wearily. 'Well, I suppose you'd better start by telling me what the arrangements are concerning meals,' she declared, shedding the jacket of her suit into Nuzab's waiting hands. By doing so, she revealed the white shirt with its frilled jabot beneath, and it was a little disconcerting to have Nuzab gazing at it with evident fascination. 'Perhaps I will take a bath, after all,' she decided, accompanying her request with a reluctant smile. 'It may help. I am feeling rather—abused!'

'Abused, lady?' Nuzab obviously did not understand what this meant, but before Ashley could bring herself to explain, another voice interrupted them.

'She means—she is tired, Nuzab,' Alain's brusque tones were harsh and unexpected. 'You may leave us, little one. Run your mistress's bath. She will join you presently.'

The peremptory note in his voice infuriated Ashley, and she swung round on him angrily, prepared to do battle. How dared he walk in here unannounced, and behave as if she was just another slave to command! She was not a servant. She was a human being, with her own will and determination, and Nuzab should not get the impression that he was welcome here.

'What do you want?' she demanded, facing him aggressively, and Nuzab, making a low obeisance, darted a startled glance up at them. 'I do not recall inviting you into my salon, *monsieur*, and I'd be grateful if you'd leave me to make my own arrangements!'

Alain's hard features registered his anger, and Nuzab, caught between their conflicting personalities, hurried towards the door. But not before Ashley had seen the warm admiration in her eyes as she gazed at the man she regarded as her master, and Ashley's resentment ignited at this meek display of sympathy. No wonder the Gauthiers had such an inflated opinion of themselves! With unsolicited supplication like this, how could any man retain a sense of proportion?

'Wait, Nuzab!' she burst out impulsively, and the Arab girl halted with evident reluctance. 'Don't bother running me a bath,' she added, maliciously enjoying the other girl's confusion. 'I've changed my mind. I'll take a shower instead.'

Nuzab's small face was a picture of anguish, and although Ashley consoled herself with the argument that she would not allow herself to be used as a pawn by either Alain or his father, she nevertheless felt incredibly mean for using the Arab girl in this way.

However, Alain brought the sparkle back to Nuzab's eyes when he abruptly endorsed Ashley's decision, and with a complaisant wave of his hand, he said: 'Miss— Conway will doubtless change her mind a dozen times, as Englishwomen are prone to do, little one. Just follow her instructions, and do not question if they sometimes contradict themselves.'

'*Aywa, Said.*' Nuzab bowed low once more, and with another anxious look at Ashley, quickly left the room.

With her departure, Ashley felt curiously bereft, left as she was to face the wrath of the blue-eyed infidel in front of her. Right now, she did not feel equipped to deal with Alain, and she turned from him abruptly and crossed to the windows with short jerky strides.

That he had followed her, she was unaware, until his hands descended on her shoulders, and he swung her round to face him with not ungentle determination. 'I would advise you not to repeat the little exhibition you have just enacted!' he declared flatly, folding his arms across his chest once he had her undivided attention. 'There are limits even to my patience, and while I am prepared to allow that you are perhaps—hurt, and angry, after your interview with my father, I cannot permit you to make a fool of me in front of the servants.'

Ashley sucked in her breath. 'And how will you prevent it?'

Alain sighed. 'There are ways, believe me, there are ways,' he assured her dryly, and her nostrils widened a little in recognition of his influence here.

'Well, you had no right to come into my apartments without invitation,' she persisted, weariness undermining her aggression. 'I thought these were the women's quarters of the palace. I thought I was protected here.'

Alain's mouth compressed. 'You insist on provoking me, do you not?' He shook his head. 'Very well. These are the women's quarters of the palace, and were my father or my brother to find me here, they would not approve. But I wanted to see you, and Nuzab knows better than to betray my whereabouts.'

Ashley put an unsteady hand to her throat. 'I suppose you wanted to see the devastation your father had wrought,' she exclaimed bitterly. 'Well, as you can see, I am still in one piece, and fully prepared to go through with this, even if it kills me!'

'You are tired and hungry, I understand this,' Alain informed her quietly. 'And I appreciate that my father is not the most tactful of men——'

'Tactful! *Tactful!*' Ashley almost choked then. 'He—he

is a tyrant, and—and a bigot, and if I never see him again it will be too soon for me!'

'*Ashley!*' Alain's face burned with a dull colour. 'I will not permit you to insult any member of my family, and most particularly not my father——'

'Why not?' Ashley's hands clenched at her sides. 'He doesn't appear to share your inhibitions about me! What have you told him? Where did he get his information? What kind of a creature did you make me out to be?'

Alain's expression hardened. 'I do not propose to discuss your previous relationship to this family.'

'Oh, don't you?' Ashley's weariness was being displaced by cold resentment. 'But perhaps you know why your father imagines I only married Hassan for his money, and why the fact of my son's conception seems totally irrelevant to him!'

'The two things are not compatible,' retorted Alain harshly. 'You married Hassan because *I* had discovered the fickle creature you were, and because his attentions flattered you——'

'*No!*'

'—and you were determined on a course of revenge!'

'I was pregnant!' Ashley protested, but Alain's lips curled in contempt.

'You were not pregnant, Ashley! Hassan did not touch you until that night I found you together, and ten days is not long enough to confirm such a supposition.'

Ashley's lips trembled. 'You won't listen to me, will you? You would never listen to me!' she cried, and Alain expelled his breath in unwilling agitation.

'I do not wish to discuss this with you, Ashley. It is over. It is in the past. Hassan is dead, and nothing you say or do can bring him back. I did not come here for this reason. I came to speak with you, to explain your situation here——'

'Oh, I understand my situation all right,' Ashley retorted tremulously. 'Your father made it perfectly clear. He wants me out of the palace, out of Khadesh, out of Murad, if it's humanly possible, and he doesn't care what means he uses to achieve it!'

'You are overwrought,' declared Alain flatly. 'And I fear my father is not yet in a mood to be discreet.'

'Discreet!' Ashley caught her breath. 'He accused me of marrying Hassan for his money, and went on to insinuate that I'd had some hand in his death! In God's name, how can you stand there and plead his cause, when you know none of it is true? I've never touched a penny of your money. I wouldn't even take it when you offered it to me! For mercy's sake, tell him I don't care about your oil wells, only about my son!'

Alain drew a deep breath. 'It is about Hussein that I wished to speak with you.' He unfolded his arms and pushed his thumbs into the low belt of his pants. 'You will meet him tomorrow.'

'So your brother told me.' Ashley made a sound of derision. 'I suppose I should be honoured that Tariq was sent to meet me. Didn't he find it odd that a prince should be despatched to meet a *governess*?'

'My brother does as my father tells him,' retorted Alain stiffly. 'And in the circumstances, it seemed a suitable arrangement.'

Ashley shook her head. 'So much ceremony! I should be flattered—bearing in mind how *flattering* you Gauthiers can be,' she added provokingly, and Alain's brows descended.

'Tariq offended you in some way?' he demanded, his eyes narrowed and intent, and Ashley heaved a sigh.

'Only to the extent that all you Gauthiers are offensive,' she declared. 'You all believe you're God's gift to womanhood.' Her lips twisted, and she added with self-mockery: 'Can you blame me if my head was turned?'

'What do you mean? What did Tariq say to you?' Alain demanded violently. 'If he has insulted you in some way—if he has insinuated that your position here is in any way suspect——'

'Well, it is, isn't it?' Ashley pointed out tautly. 'Suspect, I mean. He probably thinks I'm your mistress, and your coming here can only heighten that supposition.'

'I do not give a cent for Tariq's suppositions,' declared Alain harshly. 'And he, like you, should know better than to question my behaviour. If, however, at any time either now, or in the future, Tariq—or anyone else, for that matter—gives you any trouble, I want you to promise that you will tell me immediately.'

Ashley gasped. 'And what will you do?' She gave a mirthless little laugh. 'I've just told you that your father has virtually accused me of being a—well, you know what I mean, and you have just ignored it!'

'My father is old. He is disturbed by what has happened.' Alain pushed back a strand of his hair that had strayed with disturbing attraction across his forehead. 'You must give him time. This is not easy for him.'

Ashley bent her head. 'I think you'd better go.'

'Not yet.' Alain paced restlessly across the room to where a vase of long-stemmed blossoms drooped over a gilded screen. 'It is necessary that you should understand how you will be expected to behave here, and——' he held up a hand to silence her, as she opened her mouth to protest '—what will be expected of you, in regard to Hussein's education.'

Ashley made an involuntary gesture. 'I do know about teaching, *monsieur*,' she exclaimed tensely. 'What more is there to say? I have given you my word that Andrew shall not learn of his identity from me.'

'That name—Andrew; you must forget it,' Alain determined, and Ashley adopted a stubborn look. 'I do not know why you use it,' he continued. 'You have never had charge of the boy.'

'It was the name I called him before he was born,' she replied, running an unknowing hand over her flat stomach. 'He will always be Andrew to me, whatever Islamic names you give him.'

'The boy is a Christian, as well you know,' retorted Alain curtly, pacing across the room once more. 'Do not forget the terms you negotiated. Unlike you, I do not break my promises.'

Ashley made no response, although the sudden passion

in his voice aroused her inner indignation. What was the use of arguing with him? She never won. And now that she was here, in Khadesh, she had no reason to arouse those other emotions he had proved himself capable of displaying.

'So.' Alain halted in the centre of the floor, his feet slightly apart on the silky strands of the rug. 'You will call the boy Hussein, and he will address you as Mademoiselle.'

Ashley steeled herself not to show her feelings. 'Wouldn't—*Prince* Hussein—be more in keeping?' she enquired tautly, and Alain's lean features grew sharply defined, as he struggled to contain his growing frustration.

'Hussein will do,' he informed her sharply, raising both hands to grip his shoulders, flexing the muscles of his spine, and releasing a little of his tension. 'To the other matter of your position here, it is necessary that I advise you that you will not be permitted to leave these quarters unaccompanied——'

'What!' Ashley was horrified now, but Alain went inexorably on.

'Women are not allowed to roam the palace unescorted. You might conceivably stray into the male apartments——'

'And that would never do, would it?' she burst out hotly. 'What are you saying, Alain? What am I supposed to do? Remain here in these rooms indefinitely? You can't be serious. I—I'll go mad!'

Alain controlled his expression, and looked about him indifferently. 'You are not happy here? These rooms are not to your liking? You would prefer others?'

'Damn you, no! Yes! I mean—oh, Alain, what am I to be? A prisoner?'

His eyes darkened. 'You will be treated with the same respect reserved for all the members of my father's household,' he replied bleakly. 'You forget, this is not England. This is Murad. Here you obey our laws, our customs.'

'So I am a prisoner!' she exclaimed, unable to hide the

tremor in her voice. 'I wondered why I'd been given such splendid accommodation. Now I know. This,' she spread her arms to indicate all the rooms of the apartment, 'is the whole sphere of my existence! My world, condensed to four rooms!'

'Ashley, the same is true of my mother and my stepmother,' he told her, his voice showing some strain now. 'For God! You are as fortunate as they are!'

'Am I? Am I really?' Ashley's eyes were unnaturally bright. 'But I might not consider them particularly fortunate either.'

'You will do as you are told,' intoned Alain roughly. 'I thought all you wanted was to be with your son!'

Ashley paled a little under his savage scrutiny, and her hands trembled as they sought to pluck at the collar of her shirt. 'Very clever, Alain,' she complimented him tremorously. 'Of course, that is why I'm here. And if I object to the circumstances, I am free to leave, aren't I? Any time I want.'

'That is your decision,' he retorted, and as if unable to stand any more of this double-edged conversation, he made for the door. 'You will eat your meals in your apartments, unless you are advised otherwise,' he stated formally, pausing in the doorway, one long-fingered hand supporting his weight against the curved arch above him. His attitude tautened the buttons of his shirt across his chest, and exposed more of the fine dark body hair, but he seemed unaware of it. 'So far as your lessons with Hussein are concerned,' he continued, 'you will be taken to the schoolroom at nine o'clock tomorrow morning, and Muhammed will be there to explain what is required of you.'

'Thank you.' Ashley's tongue probed her upper lip. 'But couldn't I—I mean, isn't it possible for me to speak to Andrew tonight?'

'Hussein will await your presence at nine o'clock tomorrow morning,' Alain repeated, his expression unyielding, and withdrawing his hand, he gave her a stiff bow. '*Au revoir, mademoiselle*,' he intoned politely, and she covered her ears with her hands as his booted feet rang across the tiled floor of the room beyond.

Almost instantly, Nuzab reappeared, inspiring in Ashley the certain belief that the girl had been listening to their exchange. Had Alain known that? Was he used to the familiarities of his servants? Or was Nuzab in the pay of Prince Ahmed, a willing spy, in the camp of the enemy? At a time when Ashley was already feeling sick and vulnerable, and desperate for solitude to lick her gaping wounds, the Arab girl's smiling deference was abrasive, and she had to fight back the desire to strike the complacent expression from Nuzab's face.

'Lady like to take bath now, please?' the girl enquired, her deft hands already darting towards Ashley's clothes, and Ashley stepped backward, quelling Nuzab's eager ministry with a shake of her head.

'Thank you, if I want a bath, I'll take one,' she declared, only wanting Nuzab to go, and then knew a sudden pang when the Arab girl assumed a wounded expression. 'Honestly,' she added, feeling obliged to make some explanation, 'we don't have—servants, where I come from. It—it's very kind of you to offer your assistance, and I appreciate it, but believe me, it's not necessary.'

Nuzab gazed at her, as if she had suddenly raised the sword of Damocles above her. If the girl's face was anything to go by, she was innocent of anything except a desire to please her mistress, and although Ashley wanted to be rid of her, she was beginning to realise it was not going to be that simple.

'You do not like Nuzab?' she asked suddenly, linking her fingers together and pressing her thumbs to her lips, almost in a gesture of supplication. 'Nuzab not please you?' She gazed at Ashley, her calf-like brown eyes filled with tears. 'Muhammed will beat Nuzab if she displeases you, lady.'

'Oh, no!' Ashley stared at her in total disbelief. 'You can't be serious!'

'Master bid Nuzab care for you, lady,' she insisted,

with downbent head. 'If lady not find Nuzab pleasing——'

'This is the twentieth century, Nuzab, not the twelfth,' Ashley exclaimed impatiently. 'You're talking nonsense! No one's going to beat you. Believe me, you have nothing to fear.'

'You let Nuzab help you, lady?' Nuzab's dark eyes darted upward again, and Ashley knew a helpless sense of frustration. She couldn't honestly accept that Muhammed still took a whip to his minions, but remembering the hawklike countenance and steely gaze of the man who had escorted her from Prince Ahmed's apartments, she did not doubt he put the fear of Allah into these girls.

'All right,' she conceded now, with resignation. 'Yes, you'd better run my bath, as you suggested. We can't have Muhammed making mincemeat of you.'

Nuzab looked slightly perplexed at her choice of expression, but her delight that her services were apparently not being dismissed was genuine enough, Ashley decided. With a little bob, the Arab girl scurried out of the room, and by the time Ashley had followed her into the bedroom, there was the sound of running water emanating from the bathroom next door.

Seconds later Nuzab appeared again, carrying a cream silk robe, exquisitely embroidered in threads of gold and scarlet. Ashley, who could see her suitcases still packed at the foot of the bed, and who knew in any case that she possessed no such garment, gazed in some bewilderment at the exotic creation, and was scarcely aware of what Nuzab was doing until the cooler air of evening brushed featherlike across her breasts.

'Nuzab!' she exclaimed then, gathering the unbuttoned sides of her shirt together, and drawing back from the girl in automatic revulsion, but the Arab girl was not deterred.

'Come,' she invited, holding up the robe. 'Take off the shirt and put on the robe. Then Nuzab help you to undress.'

She smiled encouragingly, but Ashley was uneasy. 'That's not my robe, Nuzab,' she pointed out briefly, making no move to obey her. 'And I'm perfectly capable of taking off my own clothes. I'm not a child, Nuzab. I can perform simple functions.'

She doubted if Nuzab understood half of this, as her smile remained in place. 'Put on the robe, lady,' she persisted, holding it in readiness, and realising she was being unnecessarily coy, Ashley turned her back, took off the shirt, and hastily slid her arms into the sleeves of the cream gown.

'Who does it belong to, Nuzab?' she exclaimed, after it was secured about her, and the Arab girl smiled her satisfaction.

'My lady, the Princess Hélène, she sent it for you,' she replied, gesturing towards the bathroom. 'The bath is almost ready, lady. Please to come with me.'

The bathroom was the most opulent apartment Ashley had ever seen. The sunken bath was deep and round, and presently filled with soapy water, bubbling up the sides and fragrant with attar of roses. The taps and fittings were all gold, there was a gold rim to the bath and the basin, and the shower cubicle was almost completely made of gold-tinted glass. The floor was marble, and the walls were mirror-lined, and in the area surrounding the bath itself there was laid out an assortment of coloured jars and flagons containing oils and lotions and other cosmetic preparations.

Nuzab attended to the taps as Ashley bent to examine the bottles, sniffing their contents and inhaling their sweetness with a sense of having stepped back in time. In just such a way must Scheherazade have prepared herself for the Sultan, and Ashley by no means liked the accompanying connotation.

Straightening, she found Nuzab waiting to attend her, and exasperation overwhelmed compassion. 'Thank you, Nuzab, I can cope from now on,' she assured her shortly, and walking to the door, she stood beside it, her meaning plain. Nuzab looked as if she was about to argue, but then made a little gesture of assent. With another bow, she returned to the bedroom, and with some relief Ashley closed the bathroom door.

There was no way of locking it, she found, and once more uncertainty frustrated her. But her own weariness and the deliciously-perfumed steam from the tub were persuasive, and eschewing her inhibitions, she took off the rest of her clothes. The robe she removed last of all, folding it neatly and laying it on a clothes basket woven of reeds. It was quite the most beautiful garment she had ever possessed, and now that she could view it objectively, she determined that she must thank Alain's mother for it at the earliest possible opportunity. *Alain's mother!* She quivered for a moment as she stepped down into the scented suds. Who would have imagined she would meet her husband's stepmother in such strange and unreal circumstances?

The water was soft and soothing, and came up almost to her shoulders, concealing her body beneath a veil of soapy bubbles. It was hot, too, but not excessively so, just enough to relax her muscles and induce a dreamy sense of inertia. She wondered sleepily whether there was some kind of narcotic in the water, put there to create this state of lethargy. But the computations of these thoughts were too great for her to consider, and she gave herself up to the insidious delights of sensual indulgence.

Nuzab's reappearance a few moments later aroused no more than a mild irritation, and when the Arab girl knelt beside the bath and began to soap her arms and shoulders, Ashley made no real protest. She felt too languid, too quiescent, and why should she object, when Nuzab's agile fingers did the job so much more satisfactorily?

By the time Nuzab helped her out of the bath, Ashley's whole body felt suffused with warmth and relaxation. Her hair had been washed, and gleamed dully, a cause for admiration in the Arab girl, who had exclaimed over its blonde softness. Her own hair was black, and oiled, and confined in a thick braid, but when Ashley's was loosened, it hung straight and shining, and soft as silk.

Nuzab towelled her body dry with soft fluffy towels, and after perfuming her skin with a scented lotion, replaced the cream silk robe. Then, inviting Ashley to follow her, she went back into the bedroom and produced a modern hair-dryer, settling her mistress on a cushioned ottoman, before proceeding with her task.

By this time, the sense of well-being Ashley had experienced in the bath was dispersing, and the memory of Nuzab's ministrations filled her with distaste. How could she have allowed the girl to bathe her and oil her skin? She wasn't an Arab, she was English, and she couldn't believe she had permitted the girl such liberties. There must have been some mild intoxicant in the water, there was no other explanation, and with an impatient lunge she snatched the hair-dryer out of Nuzab's hands and continued with the task herself.

Nuzab hesitated for a moment, and then, apparently growing accustomed to the English girl's temperamental attitude, she bowed low and declared she would go and attend to the emptying of the bath. She went away with a smug smile still resting on her delicate features, and Ashley felt like hurling the hair-dryer after her. But she didn't. Instead, unwelcome tears pricked at the backs of her eyes, and she felt a sudden sense of misgiving. What was she doing here, she asked herself bitterly, if not destroying for ever any normal chance of life for herself?

CHAPTER SIX

BREAKFAST was brought to her at eight o'clock, and Ashley, who had had an extraordinarily good night's sleep, looked with more enthusiasm at the food. The night before she had been too troubled and upset to feel any great enthusiasm for Egyptian caviar, or *shish-kebabs*, served on a bed of fluffy white rice. Even the sticky sherbet that followed was by no means to her taste, and she had ignored Nuzab's disapproving countenance and drunk several cups of coffee, in lieu of the meal. But this morning she felt brighter, and infinitely less distraite, and even Nuzab's benign features did not irritate her today.

The bed had been superbly comfortable, but that had not really been surprising. It was an enormous thing, hung about with a tasselled canopy and spread with sheets and coverings of purest silk. Ashley had never slept between real silk sheets before, or buried her head in real feather pillows, and the gold-patterned quilt was so wide and heavily embroidered it trailed its fringe on the Turkish carpet.

Nuzab set a tray with legs across her, after Ashley had propped herself up on her pillows. It contained a warming dish of croissants, butter, cooled with cubes of ice, and thick cherry conserve, in a cut-glass container. There was freshly-squeezed orange juice, and a pot of coffee, and thick cream in a bone china jug.

'It is to your liking, lady?' Nuzab ventured, standing back with hands folded as her mistress examined the meal, and Ashley gave a half rueful nod. The night before, she had been quite unkind to the Arab girl, and now she felt contrite. She had only, after all, been doing her duty, and Ashley should not criticise her if she did it rather too assiduously.

'It looks delicious,' Ashley said now, indicating the

77

tray. 'Thank you, Nuzab. I'm very grateful.'

'Is no trouble,' Nuzab assured her softly, her smile back in place, and after hesitating a moment to touch Ashley's two long braids with a wondering hand, she disappeared into the salon while her mistress enjoyed her meal.

The previous evening, Nuzab had unpacked her suitcases, and after she had eaten a crisp croissant, thickly spread with cherry conserve, and drunk two cups of the aromatic French coffee, Ashley slid energetically out of bed. She paused a moment to wonder whether there might not have been a sedative in the cup of hot chocolate Nuzab had brought her just before she retired for the night, which would account for the dreamless sleep she had enjoyed, but whatever, this morning she felt rested and alert.

Passing the long cheval mirror that reflected the strengthening rays of the sun, Ashley lingered a moment to gaze at her reflection. What would Andrew—*Hussein*—make of her? she wondered, realising without conceit that she looked scarcely old enough to have a seven-year-old son. Had he ever pictured his mother and what she might have been like, or had he accepted that she had been some unknown Arab girl his father had briefly married? Whatever his opinion, she meant to find out for herself, if only to satisfy that ache inside her that motherhood had left.

It was already getting quite warm, and after Ashley had washed her face and cleaned her teeth, she slid back the doors of the air-conditioned wardrobes and examined their contents critically. She had thought she might wear the grey skirt and white blouse she would have worn in England, but it was obviously going to be too hot to wear anything so formal. Instead, she chose a lime-green cotton shirtwaister, with elbow-length sleeves and a swinging skirt that displayed the slender length of her legs to doubtful advantage.

She was buckling high-heeled sandals on to her feet when Nuzab reappeared, and she seemed taken aback to find her mistress had managed without her. She could not know that that was why Ashley had hurried her breakfast, so that she could be dressed and ready before the Arab girl returned.

'You have brushed your hair, lady?' she enquired disappointedly, touching the neatly-coiled chignon Ashley had adopted, and the English girl nodded.

'Yes, thank you. It's cooler worn this way. Now perhaps you will show me the way to the schoolroom.'

Nuzab shrugged, but she had no option, and after a swift glance at her wrist watch had assured Ashley it was only a quarter to nine, they left the apartments. The corridors Muhammed had hurried her along the night before were now bright and sunlit, with shafts of gold across the veined marble floor. There was the hum of activity as the servants went about their work, keeping the palace in its immaculate condition, and the warmth of a heightening temperature to bring a film of perspiration out all over Ashley's body. Through the narrow windows she glimpsed the gardens which the night before had been bathed in shadow. Now their lushness and colour seemed almost painful to the eye, a fitting setting for so much magnificence. She realised that if she had given any thought to her son's whereabouts, she had pictured nothing like this, and she could not help recognising that nothing she could give him could aspire to his father's inheritance.

It was impossible to decide where the woman's apartments ended and her son's began. But presently they approached double doors that led into a sunlit apartment, with murals of birds and animals adorning the walls. Beyond this room was another, and another, and Ashley's preconceptions of her son's enforced confinement gave way to the reality.

He had almost a whole wing of the palace to himself, and as they progressed through reception rooms and salons, playrooms and nurseries, Ashley began to appreciate how limited her ideas had been. The boy had every material thing a child could wish for, from toys of

every kind to his own private cinema, with a library of
films to rival a television station. He had his own small
library of books, his bedroom was as opulent as hers, but
as she followed Nuzab from one luxurious apartment to
another, she couldn't help wondering who he shared it all
with. Was he alone here? Did he have playmates? Or, as
Hassan was dead and Alain had not married, was he
guarded as the heir to his grandfather's wealth would be
guarded?

And there were guards about, surreptitiously to be
sure, but stationed at intervals, ostensibly to guard the
doors. Their expressions were enigmatic as they permitted
the two girls to pass, but Ashley could imagine their reaction if she, or anyone else, attempted to harm the boy.

Just when Ashley was beginning to wonder where the
child was, they emerged from the palace into a pergola-
hung court, where her son was seated in the sunlight, on
the rim of a tiled fountain, tossing crumbs to a flock of
white doves that fluttered down from the roof. He was
not alone. The man Muhammed stood to one side, in the
shadows, and Nuzab bowed low as she spoke to him in
their own tongue. Evidently she was excusing herself now
that her task was completed, and the tall Arab inclined
his head briefly and gave her permission to leave them.

The boy had jumped down from his perch at their
appearance, and Ashley saw to her relief that he was
wearing the shirt and shorts of the suit he had worn to
come to the school. He now stood staring at her with
intelligent eyes. 'You are the lady we saw in London!' he
exclaimed, reminding her of the first occasion she had
seen him, and a lump filled Ashley's throat as she
struggled to reply.

'Yes,' was all she could manage as he came eagerly
towards her, and he smiled his friendly smile, that was so
absurdly like his father's.

'I am most happy to meet you, *mademoiselle*,' he greeted
her politely, and Ashley took the hand he offered with a
feeling of utter helplessness. His skin was so soft, she
thought tremulously, wanting to raise his hand to her face

and press her lips against those small knuckles. But all that was permitted was the briefest of salutations before Muhammed came to stand beside them, and the boy turned eagerly to address him.

'You have met Mademoiselle Conway, Muhammed?' he asked, his English as good as Alain's, with only the faintest trace of an accent, and the tall Arab gave a brief nod of assent. 'She is going to teach me,' Hussein continued with enthusiasm. 'Uncle Alain told me so.' He turned back to Ashley, to include her in his conversation. 'Muhammed teaches me how to use a sword.'

'Does he?'

Ashley struggled to contain her emotions. The idea of her small son crossing weapons with the tall, hawklike Muhammed was another thong to beat herself with. But she managed to suppress her consternation, and Muhammed suggested, in heavily-accented English, that Hussein should show his new tutor where they were to work.

The schoolroom adjoined one of the many playrooms, and was furnished, like the rest of his apartments, with great attention to detail. As well as desks for Hussein and herself, there were various aids to teaching, like the computerised blackboard, that never needed wiping, and the video-cassette recorder, with its comprehensive store of tapes.

'Prince Alain had the schoolroom equipped by a professional designer from London,' Muhammed explained, as Ashley gazed in some confusion at this new concept in education, and she spread her hands a little bewilderedly at the various consoles and instruments.

'Am I needed?' she asked herself, half inaudibly, but Muhammed heard her and came to stand near her.

'You have doubts, *mademoiselle*?' he asked, his dark eyes intent, and Ashley bestowed on him a tight smile.

'Wouldn't you?' she countered stiffly, suspicious of his attentions, and he tipped his turbanned head on one side as he fingered the cord at his waist.

'Perhaps,' he conceded, watching Hussein playing with

a coloured globe that revolved electronically. 'But Prince Alain brought you here. He would not have done so if he did not think you were needed, *mademoiselle*.'

Ashley gasped, never expecting approval from the dour Muhammed. 'But you know why I'm here,' she protested, and his lips curled back to reveal large yellow teeth.

'You are here because my master wills it so,' returned Muhammed insistently, and Ashley gazed at him in amazement.

'Your master? But Prince Ahmed——'

'Prince Alain is my master, *mademoiselle*!' he retorted, making a polite obeisance. '*Saida*, Miss——Conway. I will leave you to your task.'

Hussein joined her as soon as Muhammed had departed, and looked up at her thoughtfully. 'You have green eyes!' he exclaimed, disconcerting her anew. 'My eyes are green, too.'

Ashley moved her head up and down rather jerkily. 'Yes. Yes, I noticed,' she agreed, clenching her hands to prevent herself from touching him. 'Isn't that a coincidence?'

'Uncle Alain says green eyes are——an accident of nature,' Hussein replied, quoting the words with studied accuracy. 'So we must be two such accidents, must we not, *mademoiselle*? Which means we are a little alike, does it not?'

'A little,' Ashley conceded tautly. 'Now, shall we sit down, and you can tell me all about yourself? I only know what——what your uncle has told me. And it's important that we should learn about one another, before we learn anything else.'

'All right.' Hussein was quite willing to postpone lessons until later, and they seated themselves on the stone ledge that adjoined the windows, and smiled at one another. 'You are a very pretty lady, *mademoiselle*,' he added, with a sincerity Ashley found immensely appealing. 'I am glad you have come to teach me. Uncle Alain says you were not happy at the school.'

'Is that what Uncle Alain says?' Ashley took out a

tissue and blew her nose, and then determinedly gathered her defences. 'So—you tell me what makes you happy, and about your life here at the palace.'

Hussein's small dark brows drew together. 'Very well. There are lots of things that make me happy.' He paused. 'I like swimming, and playing with my dogs. I like fencing with Muhammed.' He frowned. 'But most of all I like riding with Uncle Alain.'

Ashley licked her dry lips. 'Uncle Alain takes you riding?'

Hussein nodded. 'Whenever he can. He is a very busy man, you understand, but whenever he can find the time, we ride out into the desert.'

'Do you?' Ashley hid her apprehension. The desert seemed such a wild and dangerous place to take a small boy. 'And—and what about playmates? Don't you have any friends? Don't you have any cousins who could share your games with you?'

Hussein shrugged. 'I have cousins,' he said, and Ashley's nerves tightened.

'You do?'

'Of course.' Hussein grimaced. 'There is Kasim and Ahmed, Mara and Simone and Jalal and Selim and Hassan——'

Ashley interrupted him then. 'But who are all these cousins? I—I didn't know that your Uncle Alain had married.'

'Uncle Alain is not married,' declared Hussein sharply, and there was an underlying note of possession in his voice as he said so. 'Uncle Alain does not wish to be married. He does not need a wife to give him sons. He has *me*!'

Ashley sucked in her breath. 'And—your cousins?'

'They are the children of my aunts Media and Ramira. They do not live at the palace, as I do.' This was said without conceit, but his pride was evident, and Ashley found it difficult to proceed.

'But you do see them,' she said at last, and Hussein nodded.

'When my aunts come to stay.'

'And apart from that, you have no one?'

'I do not need anyone else,' he declared, and his expression revealed he was growing tired of this aspect of their conversation. 'Now, I have told you about me. You must tell me about you.'

'Oh, there's noothing much to tell.' Ashley made a gesture of dismissal. 'I used to teach in that school in London, that's all.'

'Do you have a family of your own?' asked Hussein doubtfully. 'Where are your father and mother?'

'They died when I was small,' explained Ashley regretfully. 'I was brought up by an elderly aunt, but she's dead now, too.'

'Then that is something else in which we are alike,' the boy exclaimed eagerly. 'My parents are dead also. They died when I was only a baby.'

Ashley's features felt frozen. 'Did they?' she breathed, and Hussein nodded.

'It was most unfortunate, but Uncle Alain was there to take care of me.' He smiled. 'I am very lucky really.'

'Yes.' Ashley could only just mouth the word, but Hussein did not seem to notice. It was obvious that so far as he was concerned, Uncle Alain was the most important person in his young life, and she felt a terrible pang at the irony of this. Alain's name was sprinkled liberally throughout the whole of Hussein's conversation, and when he went on to tell her how his uncle had taught him to swim and to ride, she acknowledged that so far as her son was concerned their relationship was the most natural thing in the world.

Later on, Hussein took her to the kennels to meet his dogs, and Ashley stood back in some confusion when two enormous hairy monsters launched themselves at him. They were Afghan hounds, she realised, when her initial shock had been contained, and for all their size and evident power they drooled around him with unmistakable affection.

'Their names are Isis and Osiris,' exclaimed Hussein, encouraging her to come closer and pat their heads. 'Do you not think they are beautiful? They were my grand-father's gift to me.'

'Not your uncle?' asked Ashley, rather dryly, unable to prevent the veiled taunt, but Hussein only smiled.

'They come with us, when my uncle takes me riding,' he conceded, pushing away their eager tongues as they sought to lick Ashley's hand. 'Behave yourself, Osiris, or Miss Conway will not want to see you again.'

Ashley shook her head. They were beautiful creatures, their coats long and silky, and of an attractively creamy shade. She could quite see that given time, she could become attached to them, too, and she guessed that for all his assertion of self-sufficiency, Hussein welcomed their companionship.

The morning passed all too quickly, and Nuzab's reap-pearance signalled the end of lessons for that day. Ashley could hardly believe it was already one o'clock, and judg-ing by Hussein's expression, he, too, regretted that their time together was over.

'I will see you again tomorrow, will I not?' he ex-claimed, once more under Muhammed's watchful eye, and Ashley fought back the foolish tears.

'Of course you will,' she assured him huskily, bidding him farewell. 'Until tomorrow—Hussein. I'll look for-ward to it.'

It was hard to return to the luxury of her apartments, which, although they were luxurious, were nevertheless impersonal. It was hard too to contemplate how she was to fill her time until the following morning, without even the freedom of the palace grounds to ease her isolation.

Lunch was served at half past one, a light meal of creamy yoghurt, followed by grilled shrimps in a smooth sauce. There was fruit to finish the meal, a choice of juicy melon or apricots, accompanied by a dish of dates, but Ashley wasn't very hungry, and Nuzab tutted as she took the food away.

The Arab girl's suggestion that Ashley might like to

rest in the heat of the day had met with an impatient refusal, but after Nuzab had left her, Ashley did feel suddenly weary. Perhaps she would lie down foor a while, if only to take off her sticky clothes, she thought, and knew nothing else until Nuzab was drawing wide the curtains on to the lengthening shadows of late afternoon.

'What time is it?' Ashley exclaimed, finding her watch had stopped, and Nuzab turned to smile at her.

'It is thirty minutes after five o'clock, lady,' she replied, approaching the bed with gentle diffidence. 'And my mistress, Princess Hélène, requests you join her for the afternoon tea.'

Ashley propped herself up on her elbows. 'Princess Hélène!' she echoed faintly. 'Alain's mother?'

'Prince Alain is her son, yes,' Nuzab agreed, her eyes widening slightly at Ashley's casual use of her master's name. 'You will accept, lady?'

'Do I have any choice?' asked Ashley, somewhat tautly, but then she made a placatory movement of her hand. 'Of course. You may tell Princess Hélène I'd be delighted to accept. Just give me a few minutes to get ready.'

To her relief, Nuzab disappeared to deliver her message, which enabled Ashley to get up and dressed without assistance. After sluicing her face and hands in the bathroom, and promising herself she would take a shower later, she put on another of her summer dresses, a simple yellow cheesecloth. Its short-sleeved design exposed her arms, and she noticed that her morning spent with Hussein, both in and out of doors, had produced a slight reddening of the skin on her forearms, where the sun's rays had touched her. She would have to take care she did not become sunburnt, she thought, realising exactly how strong the ultra-violet rays must be here, in this scorching part of the world.

It took rather loonger to do her hair than she expected, and Nuzab returned before she had it securely wound into its chignon. 'Let me,' the Arab girl insisted, bidding her sit down so that she could reach the silky coils. 'It is shame to hide beauty in ugly knot. Let Nuzab fix it for you, in prettier way.'

'Thank you, Nuzab, I prefer it how it is,' retorted Ashley, getting up again, and pushing hairpins into place. 'There, that looks better. Now, are you going to show me where Princess Hélène lives?'

The Princess's apartments were only a short distance from her own, and Ashley looked about her with interest, unable to suppress a certain excitement at meeting Alain's mother for the first time. With the approach of evening, the air was cooling quite rapidly, and it could get quite cold after dark, as Ashley knew from the previous night's experience.

Her emotions were curiously mixed as she anticipated the impending interview. Remembering Prince Ahmed's behaviour towards her, she steeled herself not to be distressed by a similar attitude from his wife. But her fears were summarily eased when she was shown into Princess Hélène's presence. The woman who rose from a cushioned lounging couch to greet her was both eager and smiling, and although she wore a gauzy tunic over loose-fitting Eastern trousers, her face and her manner were totally European.

'So you are Ashley!' she exclaimed, after bestowing a kiss on each of the startled girl's cheeks. 'I so much wanted to meet Hussein's mother. Oh, do not look so surprised, *chérie*,' she added, subsiding on to the couch again, and bidding Ashley to take a seat. 'My son had to confess. Alain could never keep any secrets from me.'

Ashley sank down on to the cushioned bench opposite, as much out of necessity as choice. She should have guessed Alain would not conceal her identity from his mother, but somehow the other woman's attitude had temporarily disarmed her.

To give her guest time to recover from her disconcertment, Princess Hélène summoned her maid, and presently a tray of tea was brought for them, and deposited with great care on the low table between them.

'*Laissez nous*, Mignon,' Hélène dismissed the girl as she

would have attended to the cups. 'We will help ourselves, *merci*.'

'*Merci, madame*.' Mignon bowed low, and with her departure, Hélène looked at her guest's pale face once more.

'You did not expect it, *non?*' she said, her tone very lightly teasing. 'My dear, why should I not wish to meet my grandson's mother? Particularly when I have so few opportunities to speak with anyone other than my servants.'

Ashley had gone even paler. 'Your—*grandson's* mother?' she echoed, but Hélène was busying herself with setting out the cups and was not looking at her.

'*Eh bien*, my husband's grandson,' she corrected herself carelessly. 'All Ahmed's grandchildren I treat as my own.'

'I see.' Ashley expelled her breath a little more freely, and accepted the bone china cup Hélène offered from the tray. 'No, no sugar, thank you. And nothing to eat either. I—er—I don't think I'm quite acclimatised yet.'

Helen shrugged, and helped herself to one of the small cakes Mignon had provided. Round and sugary, they were obviously very fattening, but Hélène's eyes twinkled as she popped it into her mouth.

'Would you believe, I was once as slim as you?' she asked, flicking a crumb from her plump fingers. 'Living here, you will find, is very demoralising, calorie-wise at least, and there is so little with which to work off one's energy.'

Ashley did not know how to answer her, and Hélène accepted her reluctance to comment. In truth, Alain's mother was still a very attractive woman, and although she had obviously put on weight over the years, she was still sufficiently supple to sit cross-legged without any effort.

'You met Hussein this morning, did you not?' she continued comfortably, offering more tea which Ashley declined. 'He is a charming child, is he not?' She shook her head. 'He is delightful, and I am very fond of him.'

Ashley drew a deep breath. 'Then—then you'll understand why I wanted to come here—why I wanted to teach him——'

'But of course.' Hélène's wide mouth curved. 'Ashley, I do not blame you. You saw him—you fell in love with him! It is the most natural thing in the world.'

'Thank you.' Ashley put down her cup. 'Thank you for saying so.'

Hélène shrugged. 'Do not thank me, *petite*. It is easy for me to say. What is not so easy to understand is why you never asked to see him before this.'

Ashley moistened her lips. 'But—didn't Alain——'

'—explain?' Hélène grimaced. 'I know what he told you. But was it enough?'

Ashley bent her head. 'I had to let him go. I had no job, no money. How could I keep him?'

Hélène nodded. 'But he was—Hassan's son. Surely you could have approached his father——'

'I wanted nothing from the Gauthiers, *nothing*!' declared Ashley bitterly. 'I only wanted to be free of their influence!'

'You let them take your baby.'

'I didn't feel he was mine. Not then,' protested Ashley painfully. 'I never even saw him. I knew if I did——'

'So you allowed Alain to bring him back to Murad.' Hélène frowned. 'Were you not curious about him? All these years——'

'Of course I was curious.' Ashley rose to her feet, unable to sit still even under so sympathetic an interrogation. 'But Alain had told me—oh, they would never have let me see him. And I didn't want to see him, really. I was afraid of how I would feel.' She shook her head. 'There's no point in discussing the past. It's over!'

'But not forgotten, I think,' remarked Hélène quietly. 'You must forgive my foolish questions, Ashley, but my son's explanations have been necessarily biased.'

Ashley quivered. 'Yes, they would be.'

Hélène inclined her head. 'But now you have—how do you say it?—turned the tables on him, *non*?'

Ashley pressed her palms together. 'Do you really think so?'

'Oh, yes, I think so,' the older woman affirmed dryly. 'You have made him acknowledge your claim at last.'

'But not my identity,' put in Ashley tightly, and Hélène sighed.

'Be patient, little one. You have—what would you say?—a foothold, *non*? The thin edge of the wedge has been inserted.'

Ashley wished she could feel as certain. 'Alain may not agree with you,' she murmured, and Hélène smiled.

'Perhaps we should ask him,' she remarked, with gentle amusement. 'Here he comes.'

Ashley turned as the object of their discussions strolled into his mother's apartments. This evening, Alain was wearing a dark blue caftan-like robe, his dark hair hidden beneath a concealing *kaffiyeh*, and as his booted feet covered the floor in easy strides, Ashley realised she must never underestimate his Arab blood. He might look like a European, in European clothes, but his father's ancestry was uppermost, and therefore strongest.

His glance flicked over Ashley, then he bent beside the couch to kiss Hélène. His mother's plump fingers lingered with evident pride on his broad shoulder, then he straightened and turned to her guest, acknowledging Ashley with a perfunctory bow. His blue eyes were veiled and enigmatic, revealing none of his inner feelings, and Ashley clung for support to the marble pillar behind her, her indignation kindling beneath that cool assessment.

'Ashley and I have been getting to know one another,' his mother inserted lightly, alleviating the rather tense silence that had fallen. 'It is good for both of us to have a female *confidante*. In this house of men, it is well to have a friend.'

Alain's lips tightened. 'I am sure you have many friends, Maman,' he declared flatly. 'And I am equally sure Miss Gilbert does not expect to find friends here, among the enemy.'

'We are not her enemies, Alain!' exclaimed his mother in surprise, and her son made a deprecating gesture.

'Perhaps Miss Gilbert would not agree with you,' he remarked, returning Ashley's resentful appraisal. 'She did, after all, reject all association with this family.'

'She has told me about that,' said Hélène comfortably, her eyes shifting from her son to Ashley, and back again. 'But why do you persist in calling her Miss Gilbert? Were you not once almost as close to her as Hassan?'

Alain's eyes narrowed, and Ashley could feel the hot colour mounting up her cheeks as he considered the import of this. 'Why should you think that, Maman?' he asked expressionlessly. 'What has—our guest been telling you? That it was I who introduced them?'

'Oh, Alain, I know about that,' retorted Hélène impatiently. 'And you know perfectly well what I mean.' Her eyes sought and held his for a moment in a challenging exchange, then she turned to Ashley. 'Please—do not let my son antagonise you, *chérie*. He can be the very devil incarnate when it pleases him to be.'

'I know.' Ashley's response was low and reluctant, and although she longed to escape from this embarrassing dialogue, she was obliged, through a sense of respect for his mother, to suffer Alain's scathing regard.

'So——' His mother endeavoured to lead the conversation into less controversial channels. 'Did you visit the Embassy this morning, Alain? Have you spoken with Monsieur Davidson?'

'I have.' Her son inclined his head. 'We leave for New York on Thursday next. I shall address the committee on Friday morning.'

Ashley listened as Hélène questioned him further, about what flight he was taking, and what time he expected to arrive in the United States, and reluctantly conceded that she did not welcome the knowledge of his imminent departure. In spite of the antagonism she felt towards him, Alain was her only link with the past, and to know herself alone in the palace, with only his mother for support, was vaguely frightening.

'My son is to address a committee of the United Nations,' Hélène explained, as Ashley shifted a trifle ner-

vously, disturbed by her uneasy thoughts. 'He has in-
itiated trade negotiations between the American government and Murad, which it is hoped will raise the standard of living of our people, and provide funds for schools
and hospitals and better housing.'

'The benefits of oil,' remarked Alain dryly, aware of
Ashley's discomfort. 'Fortunately, the Americans do not
share your distaste for our industry, and by this means we
will modernise our methods, and educate our people.'

'I—I didn't say I found oil distasteful,' Ashley countered unsteadily, and Alain's lips twisted.

'The uses to which it is put, then,' he amended dryly.
'Most particularly, the power you feel is inequitable.'

'Alain, please!' His mother sighed. 'Let us have no
more of this unequal sparring. Ashley is our guest—we
should remember that. Would you treat Hussein's
governess in this way, if you had not foreknowledge of
her?'

Alain yielded the point, but his eyes were malicious.
'You cannot alter that which is unalterable, Maman,' he
remarked inscrutably. 'Your guest knows that, and so do
I.'

'You are talking in riddles,' declared Hélène, making a
sound of exasperation. She rose abruptly to her feet. 'As I
am dining with your father this evening, I suggest you
escort your—sister-in-law back to her apartments.'

Alain's eyes flickered at his mother's deliberate refer-
ence to their unacknowledged relationship, and Ashley
made a gesture of denial. 'Please—I'm sure I can find my
own way back——' she began, but Hélène would not
hear of it.

'Alain will accompany you,' she declared imperiously,
and with a farewell gesture she bade them goodnight.

Outside in the corridor the lamps had been lit, and the
shadows of evening were dark across their path. Ashley,
forced to fall into step beside her escort, knew a sense of
depression for the empty hours ahead of her, but although she glanced once or twice in Alain's direction, he
did not speak.

At the doors to her apartments, however, when she expected him to leave her, he did not, standing back as the doors were swung wide for them and then following her into the spacious reception room. The doors were closed behind them, with the servants on the outside, and Ashley confronted her husband's brother with more apprehension than enthusiasm.

'Well?' she said, making the first overture, unable to withstand the tensions of the situation, and Alain regarded her dourly before crossing to the inner door, closing it securely and thus preventing anyone from eavesdropping.

'You saw Hussein this morning,' he said, turning back to face her, and Ashley expelled her breath on a sigh.

'Yes. Yes, I did,' she conceded quickly. 'I—we spent about four hours together.'

'And?'

Alain regarded her beneath lowered lids, and Ashley felt a kindling of emotion. What did he want from her? A written report on what had happened? Or reassurance that she had not betrayed their agreement?

'We talked. He told me about himself, about his life here, about his cousins.' She licked her dry lips. 'And I told him a little about me.' She paused. 'He's obviously very fond of you, and—and I suppose I should thank you for——'

'I do not want your thanks!' Alain interrupted her harshly, plucking impatiently at the folds of his robe. 'How did he seem to you? Are you pleased with him? Does he live up to your expectations, or were you disappointed?'

'Disappointed?' Ashley caught her breath. 'Of course I wasn't disappointed. He—he's wonderful! Adorable! I—I——' With frustration, she felt the prick of tears. 'He's a credit to you.'

Alain halted in front of her. 'You mean that?'

'Yes, I mean it.' Ashley quivered. 'You—you've done a good job.'

Alain's mouth compressed. 'He does not suspect?'

'What?' Ashley could feel her colour rising again. 'That I am his mother? No! No, of course not. How could he?'

'You did not ask him about his parents?'

'No. He told me.' Ashley held up her head. 'He said they had died when he was a baby.'

Alain inclined his head in satisfaction. 'Yes.'

Ashley's lips trembled. 'I suppose they did, didn't they?' she burst out suddenly. 'His parents did die. Or at least, one of them did!'

'Ashley——'

'No. Why should I be silent?' she exclaimed, her composure snapping as her nerves stretched to fever pitch. 'The boy loves you! He worships you! Don't you think that it's cruel to treat him in this way?'

'Cruel?' Alain looked at her with hostility, but Ashley pressed on.

'Yes, cruel!' she declared. 'If—if you marry—if your wife gives you a son——'

'I shall never marry!' grated Alain savagely. 'Do not distress yourself. Hussein shall be my father's heir, I promise you that.'

'Thank you!' But Ashley's cry was bitter. 'It's nothing less than he deserves, is it? But you'll never acknowledge that!'

'*Shut up!*'

Alain moved in closer to her, his eyes aroused and dangerous, but Ashley stood her ground. In the dark blue robes and concealing *kaffiyeh*, his tanned skin accentuating his look of alienation, she knew she ought to have been frightened of him, but she wasn't. What else could he do to her that he had not already done? He had taken her love, and destroyed it; he had taken her body, and spurned it; he had taken the only positive proof of that love, and made her relinquish it. How could he harm her now?

'You try my patience too far,' he muttered, his hands curving above her shoulders, as if he would like to take hold of her and squeeze her until she cried for mercy. But he didn't. His hands balled into fists at his sides as he fought the urge to touch her, and it was Ashley who reached out to bridge the space between them.

'What's the matter, Alain?' she whispered, her hands spreading against the blue cloth. Beneath her fingers she could feel the taut muscles of his stomach, and her pulses quickened in tenor with the thudding beat of his heart. 'Are you afraid of me?' she taunted, tilting her head towards him. 'Or could it be yourself that you're afraid of? Can't you stand to hear the truth, oh, wise one? Isn't it neat enough for those rigid principles of yours?'

'Do not do this, Ashley,' he implored, his voice thick and savage. 'I realise this has been a traumatic day for you, but I warn you—do not do this!'

'Why not?' Ashley's green eyes were tantalisingly unrepentant. 'Why shouldn't I take my share of enjoyment?' Her lips curved a little scornfully. 'You may think you hate me, Alain, but you don't, and it might be amusing to see how far your absurd principles would protect you!'

'You little bitch!' Alain's violent interjection made her aware of how accurate her charge had been, but his next words thrust all sense of victory out of her head. 'I did not realise you were so desperate for male companionship!' he snapped, his expression contorted with contempt. 'If that is all you want, I can arrange it for you. There is no need for you to prostrate yourself before me——'

He broke off with an oath as Ashley's nails raked his face, scoring half a dozen scratches down his cheeks, that immediately stood out in livid contrast to his dark flesh. Outlined in red, with the blood oozing to the surface, they looked far more ugly than they were, and Ashley was hopelessly contrite as she realised the enormity of what she had done.

'Oh—I'm sorry!' she exclaimed, as he pulled off the *kaffiyeh* and used it to dab blindly at his cheeks. Without its enveloping folds, he seemed more approachable somehow, and her sense of guilt increased when she saw the spots of blood on the cloth. 'You shouldn't have said what you did,' she protested, as he gazed at her with hostile eyes, and clasped her hands together helplessly when he turned towards the door.

'*Alain* . . .' she cried appealingly, taking an involuntary step after him. 'Alain, please—won't you say you forgive me?'

'How can I ever forgive you, Ashley?' he demanded harshly, and she knew as the door slammed behind him that he was not just referring to the scratches on his face.

CHAPTER SEVEN

ASHLEY did not see Alain again before he left for the
United States. He had no reason to come to her apartments, and as she was not permitted to leave her rooms
without an escort, there was no opportunity. Besides, she
doubted Alain would want to see her after what she had
done. She could imagine how embarrassing those
scratches would be to explain, and although she consoled
herself with the thought that he had deserved them after
what he had said, she nevertheless suffered a sense of
compunction every time she considered the implications
of her action. Still, it did mean that she faced his proposed departure with more equanimity, realising that by
the time he returned she might have gained more confidence.

Her days slipped into a routine. Mornings she spent
with Hussein. She had adapted quite easily to calling him
that, and although occasionally she recalled her name for
him, generally she managed to remember that the pre-
cariousness of her position rested on her keeping to the
rules—*Alain*'s rules. Her relationship with her son was as
satisfactory as she could make it. At least there was no
friction there, and she really believed that Hussein looked
forward to the time they spent together. Of course, with
Alain's departure, Hussein became more reliant on her
for diversion, and Ashley determinedly ignored the thought
that she was only second-best. For the moment, it was
enough that she was seeing her son every day, sharing his
work and his play, and contributing something to the
developing depth of his character.

He was an intelligent child, but she had known that
straight away, and although his schooling up until now
had been conducted by his uncle and his grandfather, he

could read and write in both English and Arabic, and could speak a little French also through Princess Hélène's tuition. His mental arithmetic was less accomplished, although he had been taught how to use an abacus, and could flip the silver beads along swiftly as his fingers ran ahead of his brain. Ashley had to teach him that it was quicker to do simple sums in his head, and although he would have argued, the watching eye of Muhammed stilled his protests with a glance.

Muhammed was often present when Ashley was giving Hussein his lessons. He never said anything. He never interfered. He was there, she was sure, to report her behaviour to Alain on his return, and to ensure that her association with her son did not go beyond the bounds of a pupil-teacher relationship. But Hussein liked him and admired him, and Ashley had to admit that she preferred Muhammed's silent appraisal to that of some of the other guards, who seemed to regard her with a mixture of insolence and contempt.

Lunch was served to her at half past one, after she had returned to her own apartments. She ate alone, finding the spicy ingredients of some of the dishes she was offered rather more than she could stomach, and then she rested for a couple of hours before taking a late afternoon swim in her own pool.

The evenings were the longest, accentuating as they did her extreme isolation here, and even Nuzab's company she found was preferable to hours spent alone, gazing at the tapestries on the walls. She had brought books with her, of course, and she read, and prepared lessons for Hussein, but she was lonely, she couldn't deny it, and she wrote long letters to her friends in England, describing the palace in great detail.

Princess Hélène did not contact her again, and she assumed that her behaviour towards Alain had alienated his mother, too. It was ironic, as she had liked the Frenchwoman, and had hoped they might become acquaintances, if not friends. But Nuzab delivered no further messages, and Ashley was forced to the conclusion that curiosity and nothing else had prompted her earlier kindliness.

When she awakened in the morning, however, and anticipated the hours ahead, she knew that in spite of everything it was worth it. Just being with her son gave her a sense of fulfilment she had never experienced before, and she determined that when Alain returned she would do her utmost not to provoke him again. She wanted to stay here. Already a week had gone by, and she could not bear the thought that they might dismiss her at the end of the month. She must stop thinking of Alain as an adversary, and treat him more as an employer, at least until her position here was more secure.

She and Hussein were at the kennels one morning when they had an unexpected visitor. Already Isis and Osiris had come to regard Ashley as a friend, and the exuberance of their welcome no longer filled her with alarm. On the contrary, she had become almost as enthusiastic about them as Hussein, and she sometimes wished she had a pet of her own to keep her company.

It was Tariq who came strolling into the enclosure as Ashley and Hussein were playing with the dogs, and the two Afghans raised their proud heads doubtfully as he slapped a riding whip against his booted calf. Today he was wearing riding clothes, a well-cut silk shirt and breeches, but the inevitable *haik* concealed his hair, and flowed protectively over his shoulders.

'Good morning, Miss Conway,' he greeted her politely, although there was arrogance in the way he moved and spoke. 'Hussein.' He bowed his head towards his nephew. 'So this is how lessons are conducted in the West. I wonder what my brother will say when I tell him so.'

Ashley straightened in some embarrassment, aware that several strands of hair had loosened themselves from the knot at her nape, and that her flowered smock was crumpled and a little dusty. But she had not expected to meet another member of the family, and she had been anticipating taking a cooling shower before sitting down to her solitary lunch.

'Good morning, Prince Tariq,' she responded now, as Hussein scrambled to his feet. 'We—er—we're not having a lesson at the moment, as I'm sure you're aware. Hussein and I were just giving the dogs some exercise.'

Tariq's somewhat thin lips curved sardonically. '*Hussein?*' he echoed. 'Do you not mean Prince Hussein?'

Ashley could feel the hot colour running up her cheeks at his deliberately insolent words. He was endeavouring to humiliate her, and she realised he had not yet forgiven her for what she had said to him in the car on the way from the airport. But, instead of getting angry, she forced a polite smile.

'Your brother, *Prince* Alain, agreed that I should call Hussein by his given name,' she replied smoothly. 'Can we help you, Prince Tariq? Is there something we can do for you?'

Tariq's mouth tightened. 'You have a ready answer, do you not, Miss Conway?' he averred, as Hussein looked from one to the other of them in some confusion. 'Yes, I have a reason for being here, but I will tell it in my own time, and not in yours.'

Ashley expelled her breath unsteadily. It seemed it was impossible to achieve any kind of harmony with this family. Always she came up against aggression, of one kind or another, and she objected to Tariq's making Hussein a party to his antipathy.

'Miss Conway likes to play with my dogs, Uncle Tariq,' the boy inserted now, interrupting their silent hostilities. 'She says that in England, children keep their pets in their homes, and sometimes even allow them to sleep on their beds!'

Tariq's dark eyes glittered. 'I trust you are not advocating such behaviour to Hussein, Miss Conway,' he remarked coldly. 'Here we are more particular about with what—or with whom—we share our beds!'

Ashley was tempted to say: 'Are you?' but she didn't. Instead she inclined her head politely and said: 'Naturally, I was not suggesting anything of the sort. It is not a practice of which I approve. I was merely explaining to Hussein that different people do things different ways.'

'Oh, yes,' Tariq nodded, 'that most definitely is true.'
He paused. 'Here, for instance, it is almost unheard-of for
a boy of royal blood to have a female governess, whereas
in England women do all manner of strange things, do
they not?'

Ashley moved her shoulders. 'Women are—freer, in
my country,' she agreed levelly.

Tariq's lips curled. 'Freer—and more independent,' he
asserted. 'But with little respect, I fear.'

Ashley refused to be drawn. 'You are entitled to your
opinion, of course,' she conceded. 'But I am sure you
didn't come here just to discuss women's rights.'

Tariq looked angrily at her, but once again Hussein
interposed. 'Is Uncle Alain back?' he asked, tugging
Tariq's sleeve with sudden perception. 'Is that what you
came to tell us, Uncle Tariq? Or did Grandpapa send
you here?'

'Your grandfather did not *send* me here, Hussein,' his
uncle retorted reprovingly. 'I am not my father's messen-
ger.' He held up his head with youthful hauteur. 'As a
matter of fact, I come with an invitation for Miss
Conway, from my mother, the Princess Izmay. She in-
vites you to dine with her this evening, Miss Conway. Is
nine o'clock acceptable to you?'

There was no question that she might refuse, of course,
thought Ashley rather indignantly, as both Hussein and
Tariq watched her reactions. She had been summoned,
just as Princess Hélène had summoned her previously. It
was just that Princess Izmay had taken a few more days
to get round to it.

'Yes, nine o'clock would be fine,' she said at last, realising that she had no possible reason to refuse. Besides, it
might break the monotony of a long lonely evening, and
perhaps Princess Izmay would not prove to be as intimidating as her husband.

She spent some time that evening deciding what to
wear. What did one wear for dinner at the palace? Was it
formal, or informal? Or was she simply exaggerating the
importance of a dinner invitation that had probably been
instigated by curiosity alone?

In the event, she chose a simple pleated polyester dress. It was black, with transparent sleeves that ended in an embroidered cuff, and embroidered motifs on both bodice and skirt. The neckline was modestly demure, displaying only an inch or two of her throat and the smooth skin of her shoulders, and with her hair coiled more loosely than usual into a softly swathed roll, she knew she was looking her best.

Once again it was Nuzab who escorted her along the lamplit corridors to Princess Izmay's apartments. Ashley was getting quite familiar with the layout of this wing of the palace, and she knew that, left alone, she could have found her way without difficulty to both Hussein's apartments and those of Princess Hélène.

'It is not far now, lady,' Nuzab murmured, glancing back over her shoulder, and Ashley nodded her thanks. 'Lady look most beautiful this evening,' the Arab girl added, without ingratiation. 'You like the way Nuzab dresses your hair?'

Ashley gave a resigned smile. This evening she had allowed the Arab girl to help her, and although the coil was not exactly what Nuzab would have preferred, nevertheless it was a compromise that satisfied both of them. She and Nuzab had compromised over many things during the past week, and although Ashley felt sure she would never get used to the Arab girl's obsequious attentions, she had lost her initial embarrassment in the girl's presence. She no longer resented her innocent familiarities, and if Ashley sometimes reflected how easy it would be to become addicted to this pampered existence, she had only to think of Alain to know he would never allow that to happen.

Princess Izmay's apartments were like those of her counterpart, large and spacious, and peopled by an inordinate number of servants, or so it seemed to Ashley. Some of these young women, however, turned out to be the Princess's daughters, and Ashley couldn't help wondering whether their presence was deliberate.

Yet Princess Izmay proved not to be an intimidating

person. She was a little shy, if anything, sheltering within the voluminous folds of a tent-like robe, that swathed her head and shoulders as well as enveloping the over-indulged fullness of her body. But she smiled quite politely when Ashley was presented to her, and although English evidently did not come to her easily she endeavoured to speak in that language.

'My son tells me you come from London, Miss Conway,' she said, by way of an opening. 'It is much different from here, I think.'

'Much different,' Ashley agreed with a smile, relieved to find that here at least her identity was not in question. 'Much colder, too,' she added, settling herself on the cushioned seat which had been offered to her, and bearing the brunt of several pairs of dark eyes. Hassan's sisters, she thought, with sudden recognition. And Tariq's, too. Did Alain have any brothers or sisters? It was something she had never asked him.

'My son will join us in a few moments, Miss Conway,' Princess Izmay continued, in her laboured English, and Ashley's skin prickled.

'Prince Tariq?' she exclaimed, in some surprise, and her hostess nodded her dark head.

'I know he enjoys speaking with you, Miss Conway,' she averred, disturbing Ashley further. 'But tell me, how are the lessons with Hussein progressing? Is he an ardent scholar, this grandson of mine, or is it hard to persuade him that such things are necessary to the future heir of the Gauthier organisation?'

Ashley hesitated. Princess Izmay's three daughters, who were seated near their mother, were watching her with an intentness she would have found unnerving, had it not been for the dismay she felt at the prospect of sharing dinner with Alain's stepbrother. Tariq had made his opinion of her clear enough this morning, and she could not imagine why he might want to join them. Unless he proposed to spend the evening baiting her, she thought, and wished she had known of his intentions before she accepted the invitation.

'Is something wrong, Miss Conway?'

The Princess was gazing at her anxiously, and hastily Ashley strove for a reply. But as she did so, something else Hassan's mother had said brought the colour to her cheeks, and she was still fumbling over her words when Prince Tariq was announced.

To her surprise, Tariq was dressed in European clothes, a well-cut navy silk lounge suit, that familiarised his rather typically alien features. After bowing to his mother and offering her a greeting, he turned to Ashley with unexpected courtesy, and his smile was quite urbane as he took the hand she offered.

'You do not object if I join this predominantly female gathering, do you, Miss Conway?' he asked her politely. 'I so much wanted to make your acquaintance, outside the duties that my father thrusts upon me.'

Ashley was perturbed, but she determined not to show it. 'I didn't know you felt that way, Prince Tariq,' she murmured, as his mother and sisters chattered among themselves. 'I thought you found my attitudes annoying, and my behaviour lacking in respect.'

Tariq's thin lips tightened. 'So I do,' he retorted, lowering himself on to the cushions beside her. 'But I also find your company stimulating, Miss Conway, and that is something rather more rare.'

Ashley's dark brows arched. 'Is that a compliment, Prince Tariq?'

'If you choose to make it so,' he replied and although Ashley was relieved that he had decided not to pursue their hostilities, she couldn't help wondering if it was wise to allow this association to continue.

Even so, she could not deny that the evening proved to be quite enjoyable. It was such a change to enjoy intelligent conversation again, for once Tariq started treating her as an equal, he revealed a surprising sense of humour. He spoke of trips he had made to other African countries, to Europe and America, and even to Australia, and his anecdotes of those journeys had Ashley gurgling with laughter. His mother said little, and his sisters scarcely spoke at all, and Ashley was brought to the inevitable conclusion that this dinner party had been arranged for Tariq's benefit, and although she was flattered at his interest, she couldn't help a certain unease at his persistence.

Yet, for all that, he reminded her strongly of Alain, when he was younger. There was a certain similarity in the way each of them smiled, the fine lines that fanned out from the corners of their eyes, and the sensual twist, of their mouths. But Tariq was not Alain, and she must never forget that, or the certain knowledge that to get involved with the Gauthiers again would be courting disaster.

Nevertheless, Tariq insisted on escorting her back to her apartments when the evening was over, and bidding farewell to his mother, Ashley wondered what she really thought of the whole affair. Was she indifferent or sympathetic to her son's wishes? Did she approve or disapprove of his evident interest in his nephew's governess? And what did she see as the eventual outcome of their relationship, in this country where mistresses were regarded without disfavour? It was a troublesome consideration, and one which Ashley hoped would not become an issue in this already disturbing situation.

At her door she halted, determined not to invite him inside, and the servant guarding her door would, she hoped, preclude any prolonged discussion. 'Thank you for bringing me back,' she said, holding out her hand pointedly, and after a moment's hesitation he took it and raised it to his lips.

'Thank *you* for a most delightful evening,' he declared, with a wry expression, and she guessed he had defined her meaning very well. 'We must do this again, before too long. Or perhaps you would do me the honour of dining with me alone.'

Ashley withdrew her hand firmly. 'I don't think so, Prince Tariq.'

'Why not?' He shrugged. 'You enjoyed yourself this evening, did you not? You were not—bored or—insulted by my conversation. I have not offended you?'

'No.' Ashley was reluctant.

'Very well——'

'Prince Tariq——'

'Think about it,' he advised softly, turning away. '*Saida hamam.* Sleep well, *mademoiselle.*'

Princess Hélène invited Ashley to lunch three days later. Perhaps she had only just heard that the governess had had dinner with her contemporary, thought Ashley a little cynically, as she prepared for the meal. Certainly it was a surprise to receive the invitation after a week of isolation, so close on the heels of the earlier one from Prince Ahmed's first wife. She wondered if there was perhaps a certain jealousy between the two women still. Or did they each share an interest in their individual son's lives? Whatever, Ashley accepted the invitation without question, and permitted Nuzab to escort her there as usual.

Prince Hélène was alone, apart from the inevitable guards, on her door, and she welcomed Ashley warmly. Watching the older woman as she drew her outside on to a sunlit patio, beyond the inner doors of the apartments, Ashley could sense no antagonism in the Princess's attitude, and she wondered if she had been mistaken in imagining that her argument with Alain could not have gone unnoticed.

A long buffet table had been set beneath a striped awning, and Princess Hélène invited Ashley to help herself to some food, then join her beside the sun-dappled waters of the pool. There was a vast assortment of dishes to choose from—cold meats and salads, shellfish and spicy fish curries, meats and vegetables, served in various different ways, and light flaky pastries that melted on the tongue. There were sweetmeats, too, sugar bonbons, Turkish Delight, and fruit of all kinds, sliced and dripping with syrup.

Ashley chose one of the delicious pastries, helped herself to some salad, which was always crisp and fresh, and then settled herself on the padded bench beside Alain's mother. A patterned canopy shielded them from the worst of the sun's rays, and it was very pleasant sitting there, listening to the play of the crystal fountain. Almost unconsciously, Ashley relaxed, and her companion smiled as she offered her a glass of some sparkling liquid.

'I wish to make a toast,' she said, by way of an explanation, and Ashley's brow creased. 'Alain,' added the Princess, raising her glass. 'His trip to the United States has been most successful. He telephoned me yesterday to tell me so.'

'Oh!' Ashley's tongue circled her lips, before she allowed Princess Hélène to touch glasses. Did this mean Alain would be coming home now? And why should his mother choose to share her delight with her?

'Drink!' commanded the Princess, waiting for Ashley to do so. 'It is quite innocuous. I am not allowed to drink champagne here, but this is light and sweet, and makes a fair substitute, even if it is totally free of alcohol.'

She grimaced, and Ashley obediently brought her glass to her lips and tasted its chilled contents. It was delicious, cool and bubbly, and enabled her to say, with assumed casualness: 'Does this mean your son will be coming home, *madame*?'

'Undoubtedly,' said her companion, with evident satisfaction. 'Naturally he must report all that has happened to the government, but it seems likely that Alain will spend more time in New York from now on.'

'It does?' Ashley was appalled by her reaction to this news, but Princess Hélène did not appear to notice the girl's suddenly pale features.

'But of course. It is an honour,'she exclaimed, in answer to Ashley's question. 'As he is Murad's representative, his presence there will be essential, for some time at least, and I regret I will have to get used to being without his company.'

'Yes.' Ashley managed to articulate the word with difficulty. What then would happen to Hussein, with his uncle's departure? Of all the members of his family, Hussein would miss him most, and Ashley knew her son regarded Alain with an almost possessive fervour. She couldn't bear the thought of the boy's suffering when he learned what his uncle planned to do, and she knew that she was no substitute for what Alain had given her son.

'You are not eating.' Princess Hélène distracted Ashley from her thoughts with a playful pat on her arm. Then, as her sharp eyes observed the girl's anxious expression, she exclaimed: 'What is it? Is something wrong? There is nothing the matter with the food, is there? Or is the fruit cup not to your taste?'

'No. No. The food's fine, and—and the fruit cup is delicious,' Ashley exclaimed hastily, but Alain's mother was not convinced.

'You do not look as if anything is delicious, *petite*. You look as if you had seen a ghost. Come, drink up! I thought you would be pleased at Alain's good fortune, and pleased, too, to have your son all to yourself.'

Ashley put down her glass and her plate on the bench beside her, and folded her sweating palms together. 'It—it's about Hussein, I was thinking,' she ventured. 'He—well, he's going to miss Al—your son an awful lot.'

'Is he?' Princess Hélène raised her dark eyebrows.

'You know he is.' Ashley was desperate. 'He—he worships his—his uncle.'

'Yes, perhaps you are right.' Princess Hélène was thoughtful. 'But he will get used to it. After all, he has you now.'

For how long? thought Ashley cynically, but she did not voice her fears. How long would Prince Ahmed allow her to remain once Alain was not here to support her? She bent her head. It was the first time she had acknowledged that Alain had supported her, but how strong could that support be when he was thousands of miles away?

'Do not look so depressed, *chérie*.' Clearly, Princess Hélène had no qualms concerning her son's promotion. But then why should she have? Ashley asked herself bitterly. Hussein was only her husband's grandchild, not hers, and perhaps she still hoped that Alain might find himself a suitable wife and produce sons of his own blood. 'Come,' she added, 'finish your drink. I have a mind to take a trip this afternoon, and you shall come with me.'

'A trip, *madame*?'

Ashley was nonplussed, but Hélène only laughed. 'Along the coast road, little one,' she averred gaily. 'To Samaka and beyond. You would like that, would you not, Ashley? It will help to blow away those cares that are bringing such unbecoming lines to your forehead.'

They drove to Samaka in a chauffeur-driven convertible, with only one guard, seated beside the chauffeur. Princess Hélène swathed her head and shoulders with silken scarves, but Ashley had made no such preparations, and before long the wind had whipped her hair into wild disarray. But it was so exhilarating, and so invigorating to be outside the confining walls of the palace, that she cared little for the disorder of her hair. It was so good to feel the sun on her skin and the wind in her face, and the salty tang of the sea on her tongue.

The coast road was a little nerve-racking in places, winding through a series of hairpin bends as it approached the refinery at Zarif. But already a motorway building programme was in progress, and the dust raised by half a dozen earth-moving machines mingled with the unmistakable scent of oil.

Beyond the refinery, the road followed the rocky shoreline, dipping down into hollows where the dunes came down almost to the sea's edge, and rising again to look out over the untrammelled reaches of the desert. Miles and miles of rolling sand stretched before them, and beyond, the purple-shadowed mountains raised their peaks to the sky.

Driving back again, Princess Hélène bade the chauffeur drive through the older part of Khadesh, and she pointed out places of interest to her companion. There were mosques and museums that Ashley would like to have explored, but she contented herself with looking, and listening to Hélène's commentary.

'It is odd, is it not?' she remarked, with wry humour, as they drove back to the palace. 'Murad—or at least the area of which Murad was a part—has one of the oldest civilisations in the world. Men and women lived and worked here thousands of years before Christ was born, and yet in some ways the people have not developed at all.'

Ashley captured an errant strand of hair that had blown across her mouth, and smiled. 'Do you mean culturally or socially?'

'I think you know what I mean,' retorted Alain's mother dryly. 'It was a great wrench for me, leaving the freedom of Paris to come and live in seclusion at Kom Shar.'

Ashley frowned. 'Why did you do it, *madame*?' she asked unthinkingly, and then coloured in embarrassment. 'I mean—please, don't answer that. It was impertinent of me to ask.'

'I do not mind.' Princess Hélène shrugged her plump shoulders. 'It was a fair question. Why did I do it?' She sighed. 'I sometimes wonder myself.'

Ashley hesitated. 'How did you meet Prince Ahmed?'

'At a reception given by my father,' replied the older woman at once. 'My father was attached to the Embassy in Paris, and Prince Ahmed was a guest of the government.' She smiled. 'You can have no idea, looking at him now, how handsome he was thirty years ago. He was tall, like Alain, but much darker, of course, and he had a certain charm that I, as a romantic, responded to immediately.' She laughed. 'I suppose I had some fantastic notion of marrying a sheik and living in a tent in the desert.' She shook her head. 'The reality proved me wrong.'

'But you loved him, didn't you?' ventured Ashley tentatively, and Princess Hélène nodded.

'Yes. Yes, I loved him.' She made a regretful gesture. 'Unfortunately I was not aware of what loving him portended.'

Ashley didn't like to ask what the Princess meant by this, but as if defining her interest, Hélène went on: 'You see, I knew I was not his first wife. He had explained that to me, and the somewhat unpalatable news, I confess, that he had no intention of divorcing Izmay.' She sighed again. 'What I did not appreciate was that Ahmed should turn to her again while I was expecting our son Alain.'

Ashley's stomach contracted. 'Hasssan?' she queried, and Hélène nodded.

'Yes, Hassan was born only a few months after Alain. And Melina and Zeffira some years later.'

Ashley frowned. 'But you—you had no other children?'

'No.' Hélène was very firm about that. 'I gave Ahmed his eldest son, and that is all. Foolishly, I refused to have any more children.'

'Foolishly?' Ashley frowned.

'Yes.' Hélène expelled her breath wearily. 'Now, I realise it was a foolish thing to do. Izmay has her second son and several daughters. I have only Alain. And as he does not show any intention of getting married, I shall never have the grandchildren I crave.'

It was late in the afternoon, and the shadows were already lengthening towards evening when the gates of the Askar Palace swung open to admit them. Ashley was not sorry the journey was over. She had welcomed Alain's mother's confidences, but her remarks concerning her son had struck too close to home, and Ashley needed time to reconcile her troubled emotions.

Nuzab was not waiting when the sleek car discharged its occupants into the paved courtyard before the palace, but after Princess Hélène had bade her *au revoir*, a dark-skinned manservant escorted her to her quarters. Ashley was tired, not least because this was the first afternoon she had not taken a rest since arriving in Murad, but also because the journey had been unexpectedly exhausting. She was looking forward to Nuzab's ministrations for once, and welcoming the prospect of a relaxing bath. She realised she must look much different from the demure governess the guards were used to seeing, and judging by the occasional glances her escort kept casting her way, he evidently found the sight of so much honey-fair hair quite fascinating. Her efforts to restore it to some semblance of order had not been successful, and its weight about her shoulders was another burden tonight.

The guard left her at the entrance to her apartments, and she entered the reception room with a decidedly dejected air. The things Princess Hélène had told her earlier were now returning to disturb her, and she sighed as the doors closed behind her. Leaning back against them for a moment, she raised her hand to run it wearily over her hair to her nape, then began unfastening the buttons of her dress. It was a button-through tunic-style dress, with a square neckline and elbow-length sleeves, and underneath she was wearing nothing but cotton bikini pants. Even so, her clothes had stuck to her skin in the heat of the day, and hearing a sound from the salon, she pushed herself away from the door to go in search of her bath.

'Nuzab?' she called. 'Nuzab, is that you?' and then halted in silent horror, one hand pressed to her mouth, when a man appeared in the open doorway leading to the inner room. He was wearing Arab dress, the long djellaba that fell straight from his broad shoulders, and standing in the shadow as he was, she did not immediately define his identity. But when she did, her hand fell from her mouth and she gazed at him half angrily, as she sought to gather her composure.

'Alain!' she breathed, and she was frustratedly aware that she was trembling. 'Oh, Alain, you startled me! What are you doing here? I thought you were in New York. Your mother said she spoke to you there only yesterday.'

'She did,' retorted Alain harshly, but the inflection of his words bore little association to their meaning. 'In the name of Allah,' he exclaimed, his face flushed with a dark anger, 'cover yourself!' and she realised with sudden sobriety that she was half naked before him.

CHAPTER EIGHT

"You shouldn't be here,' she exclaimed resentfully, gathering the two sides of her dress together and wrapping her arms about herself almost protectively. 'Wh-where's Nuzab? I want to take a bath. If—if you have something to say to me, couldn't it wait until later?'

Alain moved into the room, and as he did so the light from above illuminated the hard lines of his face beneath the *kaffiyeh*. The marks her nails had made were only faintly visible now, and could easily have been excused as the results of using too sharp a razor, but the remembrance of their last interview could not be so easily erased.

'No,' he said heavily now, 'it cannot wait, Ashley. I am dining with my father this evening, and I came here at this time to speak with you before the demands of business supersede all else. I shall not have time to speak with you later.'

'Then speak to me tomorrow,' she retorted, moving her shoulders dismissingly. 'I'm hot and I'm tired, Alain, and quite honestly, I can think of nothing we have to say to one another that couldn't wait——'

'Can you not?' he grated, stepping into her path when she would have brushed past him, and gripping her arm with an iron hold. 'But then you do not call the tune here, Ashley—I do, and it is I who shall decide when we have speech, do you understand?'

Ashley refused to be intimidated, even though his fingers were digging into her flesh. It was not all that difficult when she had so many other sensations to combat, not least her awareness of his brooding magnetism, accentuated by the nearness of his body. She could imagine so well the brown-skinned limbs beneath his loose robe, the sinewed hardness of his chest, the flatness of his stomach, the muscled length of his legs. She could remember those legs covering hers, his body pressing hers down into the softness of a mattress, and the thrust of his possession . . .

Her breathing quickened, but her expression never changed. He should not see that he was hurting her, she determined, forcing all other thoughts away, and waited mutely for him to continue.

'Where have you been?' he enquired, with controlled emphasis, and she managed to answer him with equal self-possession.

'Your mother invited me to go driving with her,' she replied, holding up her head, and his expression hardened at the challenge in her eyes.

'I meant—where did she take you?' he persisted, making no move to release her, and the encroaching numbness of her arm caused Ashley to speak more recklessly.

'Don't you know?' she exclaimed. 'Didn't Muhammed tell you? I'm sure he could have done. He seems to know everything around here.'

'I am asking you,' declared Alain coldly, and Ashley's control snapped.

'Is this why you're here?' she demanded. 'To find out what I've been doing in your absence? Are these the important questions that couldn't wait until tomorrow?'

'Ashley!'

'Well——' She paid no heed to his warning admonition. 'Why have you come here? To taunt me with the news of your new position in New York? To tell me how easily you've managed to outwit me? To explain to me how difficult it will be for me to remain here after you've gone——'

'What in God's name are you talking about?' he snapped violently, releasing her to press his balled fist into his palm. 'What has my mother been telling you? What manner of greeting is this? When I come here merely to discuss my nephew's progress, and meet only anger and hostility!'

Ashley was not listening to him, however. Realising she

was free, she had brushed past him into the salon, and when he caught up with her, she was on the point of slamming her bedroom door in his face. But his booted foot prevented her dramatic departure, and he grasped her wrist angrily, swinging her round to face him. The sudden restraint caught Ashley unawares, and in trying to save herself she let go of her dress. Immediately the two sides parted to reveal the rose-tipped fullness of her breasts, the peaks hardened by her agitation and swollen by her emotions.

Alain's expression changed, and his fingers encircling her wrist slackened almost perceptibly. Ashley could have got away from him then, easily, but she didn't, she remained where she was, making no move to cover herself. She was paralysed by the darkening of emotion in his eyes, by the sallow cast of his features, and the impassioned sensuality of his mouth. She felt that if she moved, or made any attempt at withdrawal, his control might slip, and the latent strength in the fingers around her wrist could assume crushing proportions. Despite the slightly glazed expression he wore, he still had the power to overwhelm her puny efforts, and she waited, scarcely breathing, for him to make the next move.

'No,' he muttered at last, when Ashley was feeling almost faint with reaction, 'I should never have allowed you to come here.' With a savage gesture he released her arm, and his mouth compressed in bitter lines. 'By Allah,'' he choked, 'I will not let you do this to me!' and with a groan, half of contempt, he turned abruptly away from her.

He was halfway across the salon when he halted, and by this time Ashley had drawn her dress about her, and was watching him apprehensively. 'Your lessons with Hussein,' he stated, in a detached clipped tone, eloquent of the strain this was putting on him. 'They go well?'

Ashley could not speak. She was too shocked to make any immediate response to him, but as he waited she forced herself to respond. 'Very well,' she got out at last, and breathing heavily, he nodded.

'Good. There is no problem, then?'

'No.'

Ashley's voice was scarcely audible as she endeavoured to equal his constraint. She could hardly believe this conversation was taking place after the emotional events of the last few minutes, but she knew that to sustain her antagonism would gain nothing.

'I am relieved.' Alain's deeper tones were flat and expressionless. 'I will speak with Hussein myself as soon as I have an opportunity. You may tell him that, if you will. Tonight I discuss my journey with my father, and tomorrow I must give my report to the government. I do not know how long that will take, but you may assure Hussein I shall not neglect him unnecessarily.' He sighed, and there was a weariness in the way he flexed his shoulder muscles. 'That is all I came for. I will go now. *Masa-l khair*, Ashley. Good night.'

Ashley took a step forward. 'Alain——'

'*Mademoiselle!*' he retorted, with a click of his heels, and without giving her a chance to say anything more, he strode swiftly out of the room.

Ashley found it hard to sleep that night. She tossed and turned for hours, trying to find the secret of oblivion, but unable to escape the turmoil of her own thoughts. No matter how she tried, she could not put Alain's image out of her mind, or prevent the memories of the past from swamping her weakened consciousness.

The remembrance of her wedding day stood out in stark detail. She remembered how she had felt, the hopelessness she had endured, and the bitterness with which she had embarked upon that disastrous course. Would she have married Hassan if he had not had money, if he had not been Alain's brother? She had asked herself that a hundred times, and always she came up with the same answer, which was no answer at all. She didn't know. She didn't honestly know. All she really understood was that she had been hurt, terribly hurt, and desperate, and Hassan had not been the kind of man one could refuse.

He had wanted her. He had seen her, and he had wanted her. Whether or not he had loved her she doubted very much. She had been Alain's girl-friend, and Hassan had always coveted everything that was Alain's. Oh, he had hidden it well, even from Alain himself. But she had known, she had proof. Only no one, least of all Alain, would believe her.

She rolled on to her stomach, pummelling her pillow with weary fists. What's the use of bringing all this up now? she asked herself despairingly. It was over. Alain had said it was over. It was not something one could resurrect at will. It didn't matter now, none of it mattered. Hassan was dead. He had paid for his sins, and Alain would never speak ill of the dead.

But it was so unfair, she thought, burying her hot face in the soft pillow and feeling the dampness of tears against her cheek. They had been so happy, she and Alain. She had loved him so much, and she had believed him when he said he loved her. They had been so good together. Until Hassan arrived on the scene . . .

Sniffing, she rubbed her eyes with the flat of her hands, and as she did so she remembered how she had met Alain for the first time. She and Lucy Armstrong had been staying at the Foresters' apartment. Deborah Forester was a girl they had met at university, and she had invited them for the weekend. Her parents were in the Diplomatic Service or something similar, and they were giving a party and needed some extra girls. She remembered both she and Lucy had been a little apprehensive about the arrangements, but in the event it had all proved rather dull and boring. The men were all middle-aged or elderly, and the only interesting man present, a young Arab from Murad, had not paid them the slightest bit of attention.

It was quite late in the evening, when Ashley was returning from the bathroom, that she was accosted by a rather persistent gentleman, with a distinct paunch and red mottled features. He had succeeded in backing her into a corner, and short of creating the kind of scene she knew the Foresters would detest, Ashley had not known what to do. But when the man tried to press his flabby body against hers, and began fumbling with the bootlace straps of her cocktail dress, she had started to struggle, and their panting exchange attracted the attention of the young Arab, on his way to collect his overcoat.

It had all been over without a great deal of effort. Alain was taller and stronger, and infinitely younger, and the florid-faced gentleman went on his way, mopping his sweating features with his handkerchief. Ashley was left to stammer her thanks and her apologies, hoping the young man would not imagine she had invited the assault, and Alain had smilingly assured her that he had enjoyed it.

'I saw him watching you earlier,' he remarked, pulling a leather jacket on over his dark suit. 'And I saw him follow you into the hall. I suspected what he had in mind, so it was no coincidence that I happened along.'

'Well—thank you, anyway,' Ashley stammered. 'I'm very grateful.'

'Think nothing of it,' Alain told her, and took his departure before she could think of any way to detain him.

She had thought that would be the last she saw of him, but it wasn't. A week later he turned up at the college where she was studying, and invited her to have lunch with him, and although Lucy was rather doubtful about his Arab background, she had to admit he was attractive.

Looking back now, Ashley could see how gullible she had been. She had been such an easy target, she realised, and Alain's approach had been so practised, it made the fat man's at the party look like that of an amateur. From the beginning, he must have known how she felt about him, and how her skin tingled every time he took her hand. She had never realised she had such a sensuous nature, until Alain began to play with her emotions, and once it was ignited, she had no way of controlling it.

It took him a week to get her into his bed, and possibly half that time for her to be so madly in love with him that she could think of nothing else. She, who had always scorned other girls for their promiscuity, no longer had control of her own life. She ached when she was away from him, with a physical hunger that no one else could assuage. She yearned for the warm possession of his mouth, she craved the urgent demands of his body, and she died a little every time something happened to prevent their meeting. She would have done anything for him—left her friends, her career, anything—just to be with him. Time had no meaning when they were apart, and she had really believed he felt the same. Certainly she had had no doubts that she could arouse him as no other woman had been capable of doing. Why else did he neglect his work to be with her, taking her to his apartment high above Regent's Park, and teaching her all there was to know about the relationship between a man and a woman? He had seemed incapable of staying away from her, and if his work at the Gauthier building had suffered in consequence, it had not troubled him then.

It was perhaps two months into their affair when Hassan came on the scene. Hassan, who had been sent by his father to work in the London office, and who lost no time in destroying all the trust they had in one another. His was a destructive influence, carrying with it the seeds of devastation, and Ashley could still feel the desolation that his arrival precipitated. Would things have been different if he had not interfered in their lives? Would Alain have asked her to marry him, as she had anticipated? Or had Alain used Hassan's infatuation to his own ends, because their association was beginning to pall?

It was too late now to speculate on something that was so nebulous. Alain had not asked her to marry him. He had believed Hassan's story in spite of her pleas. And when Ashley found that she was pregnant, marrying Hassan had seemed like the logical thing to do. But only logical so long as she sustained her hatred towards Alain, she admitted now, and that had not lasted long after her reckless decision.

In the morning, Ashley felt dull and heavy-eyed, and Nuzab viewed her pale face with some misgivings.

'Lady not feel well?' she asked, when she brought

Ashley's breakfast tray, and it was easier to admit to a headache, than explain about her restless night.

After her shower she felt a little better, and by the time Nuzab escorted her to Hussein's apartments she had succeeded in disguising her weariness to all but the most observant eye. The last thing she wanted was for Muhammed to notice her distracted air and report its presence to his master.

Hussein was waiting eagerly for her, and after the usual greetings were over, he skipped about the patio with evident animation.

'Uncle Alain is back,' he carolled, announcing his news with dancing eyes. 'Is that not exciting, *mademoiselle?* Uncle Alain is home, and perhaps this morning he will come and take me riding!'

Ashley glanced with some trepidation at Muhammed, standing silently by the fountain, then addressed herself to her son. 'Darling, it is exciting that your—uncle is home, but don't build your hopes too high. Uncle Alain may have other matters to attend to.'

'But you do not understand.' Hussein's small face grew indignant. 'Uncle Alain always comes to see me, as soon as he gets home. He did not come last night, so——' he shrugged his thin shoulders, 'he will come today.'

Ashley did not quite know how to handle this. Somehow, Hussein had made it impossible for her to tell him that she had already seen Alain, and she looked once more at Muhammed, begging his intervention.

The hawk-faced Arab acknowledged her difficulties with a curiously wry smile, then he interposed smoothly: 'You know your grandfather demanded your uncle's presence at dinner last evening, little pigeon. I told you so.' His eyes flickered briefly over Ashley. 'Miss Conway is right. Today your uncle may have other matters to attend to.'

Hussein's small chin quivered. 'But he always comes to see me first, always!' he exclaimed, and once again Ashley felt the Arab's eyes upon her.

'Perhaps there was something more urgent that he had

to do,' he responded, his obsidian-dark eyes boring into Ashley's, and she knew without a shadow of a doubt that Muhammed knew exactly where Alain had been.

Hussein heaved a deep sigh. 'Well, I do not believe you,' he declared at last, sulkily. 'Uncle Alain loves me best. He said so. I—I am the son he has never had.'

Ashley could feel the colour draining out of her face at his words, and she prayed that Muhammed would not notice. She had no doubt that Hussein was repeating, parrot-fashion, something that had been said to him by Alain, and the pain that it evoked was impossible to avoid. It was like a knife turning savagely in her stomach, and she unconsciously wrapped her arms around her middle, as if to staunch an open wound.

'Little boys must learn to grow up,' said Muhammed firmly, and Ashley was eternally grateful for his support, involuntary or otherwise. 'Come, get your sword. Let us show Miss Conway how the son of a Bedouin chief faces his adversaries and defeats them!'

Hussein was not enthusiastic to begin with, but under Muhammed's controlled encouragement his spirit reasserted itself, and it was Ashley who watched with her heart in her mouth. The tipped foil blades could still effect injury, and she was standing with her hands pressed to her mouth when a masculine tread sounded on the tiled courtyard. She turned, instinctively steeling herself to meet Alain's hard features, but it was Tariq who hailed her with a salute from a gloved hand.

The fencing lesson was speedily abandoned, and Hussein came to greet his younger uncle with smiling anticipation. 'Did you know? Uncle Alain is home?' he demanded, wiping his face with a somewhat sweaty hand. 'Did you come to tell me when I can see him?'

'I am afraid not, Hussein.' Tariq's drawl was regretful. 'Unfortunately, I am not privy to your uncle's actions, and so far as I am aware he is at present in Khadesh, with the Prime Minister.'

Hussein's expression drooped again. 'Then why are you here, Uncle Tariq? Do you have another invitation for Miss Conway?'

Tariq's dark face flushed with unbecoming colour. 'You have too much to say for yourself, Hussein,' he retorted, his expression mirroring his impatience as he transferred his attention to the tall Arab, listening with his usual impassivity to this exchange. 'Your charge is needful of soap and water, Muhammed. See to it, will you, while I speak privately with our English guest.'

Guest! Ashley looked askance at this new interpretation of her position, but Muhammed was more used to taking orders. 'As my lord wishes,' he averred, and only Ashley sensed the gentle irony, as he took Hussein's hand and led him unprotestingly into the palace.

'So—this is better, is it not?' commented Tariq smugly, when they were alone, plucking the tender leaves from a fig tree and crushing them carelessly between his fingers. 'It is difficult to find an opportunity to speak with you, *mademoiselle*. You are either teaching Hussein, or driving with my stepmother, and I did not think you would care for me to send a message with your maid, Nuzab.'

'No.' Ashley made the polite denial, hoping Muhammed would not take too long over washing Hussein's face and hands. She had no desire for her relationship with Tariq to develop beyond the lines she had already set, and realising silence was more dangerous than speech, she hastened on: 'It was most enjoyable driving with Princess Hélène yesterday. We went to a place called Samaka, and on the way back we took the time to explore a little of Khadesh. It's a beautiful city, isn't it? One day I hope to be able to look around some of its museums; the history of the area is quite fascin——'

'Wa'if!' he broke in on her impatiently, crossing the patio to stand by her side. 'Miss Conway—*min fadlik*, I do not even know your first name!—I did not come here to discuss the architectural beauties of my country, nor indeed to discuss its museums or its history. I came because I wanted to see you, to speak with you, to gain your promise that you will dine with me again—perhaps tomorrow?'

'Oh, please——' He was going too fast for her, much too fast, and she glanced urgently towards the arched doorway through which Muhammed and Hussein had disappeared, hoping that she might see them coming back. But as yet there was no sign of them, and she was left to face Tariq's growing ardency. 'I—I don't think—I don't think your father would approve,' she temporised, moving her head decisively, but Tariq was unmoved by this appeal to his family honour.

'My father does not choose my friends, *mademoiselle*. I am not a child. I make my own decisions. And while, I admit, my family's dealings with your race have not always been enthusiastic, no one could compare you to the woman who took my brother's life!'

Ashley's lips parted. '*The woman who took your brother's life?*' she echoed with real horror, and Tariq, taking her reaction in an entirely different way, nodded complacently.

'Oh, yes,' he said, and for the moment he was diverted from more personal pursuits. 'Poor Hassan! He was Hussein's father, you understand? He also was my brother, my *real* brother, not like Alain who is only my half-brother.'

Ashley was torn between the desire to stop him there, and the equally powerful urge to have him go on. What had his father and his brother told him of Hassan's death? What construction had they placed on that brief but disastrous marriage?

She was given no chance to choose. As if enjoying her shocked immobility, Tariq continued: 'Hussein does not know this, of course, but his mother was English, like you, *mademoiselle*. Hassan met her while he was working in London—we have offices there, as you might imagine—and Hassan was always susceptible to a pretty face.' He sighed. 'She was completely unscrupulous. As soon as she realised who Hassan's family were, she determined to have him, and I regret, she used the oldest trick in the book. Hence—my nephew.'

Ashley felt too numb to respond. It was not that his

words had told her anything she didn't already know, it was simply the matter-of-fact way he said them. As if they had to be authentic. There was no room for doubt. But if Hussein ever heard those words, was ever given that explanation . . . She would stand no chance of convincing him of the truth.

Moistening her lips, she endeavoured to sound only mildly interested, as she asked: 'But—your father, Prince Ahmed. Couldn't he have persuaded your brother to change his mind? Or—or Prince Alain?'

'Ah!' Tariq threw the remains of the leaves away, and they fluttered heedlessly to the ground. 'That is something I used to wonder myself. But,' he drew a little nearer as he spoke, 'it appears that my lordly older brother was involved, too.'

'Oh?' Ashley hoped he would attribute her sudden colour to his nearness.

'Yes.' Tariq's lips curved in sensuous amusement. 'I have learned that it was because of Alain Hassan was sent to London. It was he who introduced Hassan to this—female huntress. Apparently Alain had become involved with her himself, and it was his wish that Hassan might sever the connection.'

Tariq was so engrossed in his story, he was unaware of Ashley's stiffening countenance. It was evidently a story he had related many times before, and she was appalled at the thought of how distorted it was from the truth. It was like seeing the other side of a coin, or herself in a mirror reflection. The events were there, but hopelessly misrepresented, so that roles were reversed and characters changed. But the most damning thing in Ashley's eyes was Alain's perversion of their relationship. She ought to have suspected it, of course, but until this moment she had not considered why Hassan should have chosen that particular time to join his brother in London. She remembered now, right at the start of her association with Alain, he had told her Hassan was at the university in Khadesh. She should have suspected something when he suddenly turned up in London, but she had been so blindly infatuated with Alain, she had never questioned Hassan's appearance.

'You look dismayed, *mademoiselle*,' Tariq said now, and Ashley made an effort to pull herself together.

'I—I was—surprised, that's all,' she admitted faintly. 'Don't—don't you think Hussein should be told who his mother was?'

'No.' Tariq was adamant about that. 'She's still alive, you see, this woman! She gave Hussein to us when he was just a baby, and she hasn't seen him since. I suppose Hussein has told you that both his parents are dead? Yes, well—that was the simplest explanation. After all, she didn't really want him. She only wanted money.'

'*Money!*' Ashley almost choked, but Tariq did not notice.

'Yes,' he drawled with heavy disapproval. 'So many thousands of dollars, to silence her wagging tongue, in the clear and certain knowledge she would never interfere.'

Ashley's legs felt like jelly, and she sought the rim of the fountain, sinking down upon it with shaking limbs. It was worse, so much worse than she had expected, and painful indignation burned like a flame inside her. She had been feeling sympathy for Alain, she realised. She had actually experienced moments when she had felt guilty at the way she had manipulated him. But she had not manipulated him at all. He had manipulated her, and what was more, he was going on doing it!

'Are you all right?' Tariq came to stand near her, one booted foot raised to rest on the stone rim beside her. 'You look pale.' He glanced upward at the ball of gold above them. 'It is the sun. You must be careful, *chérie*. Its rays can be deceptively powerful.'

Ashley drew an uneven breath and looked up at him. 'Like people,' she remarked, her tone unmistakably bitter, and Tariq frowned.

'*Pardon?*'

'This girl,' declared Ashley unsteadily. 'Hussein's mother, *monsieur*. You do not think perhaps she may have been dazzled by a deceptively powerful light? That she may have been burned by its remorseless rays?'

Tariq looked puzzled for a moment, then he smiled. 'Ah, I see. You make the metaphoric comparison.' He shook his head. 'But no. Spare no sympathy for her, *mademoiselle*. She knew exactly what she was doing.'

Ashley hesitated. 'But she got nothing out of it, did she? I mean——' she quivered, 'if she gave her baby away—if her husband died——'

'You forget the money, *mademoiselle*,' announced Tariq, with triumphant emphasis. 'She was well recompensed, you may be sure. My father is not a poor man, and he would give much to assure the future of his grandson.'

Ashley could not believe what he was saying. 'You— you think—Hussein's mother was *paid*!' she exclaimed tremorously, and Tariq dropped his foot to the ground as the sound of Hussein's boyish treble drifted irresistibly nearer.

'*Iman*, the boy is coming back!' he exclaimed, with evident impatience. 'And you have not yet given me your assurance that you will consider my invitation!'

Ashley got to her feet with some misgivings, but the sight of her son was a potent restorative. What could she expect, after all? she asked herself bitterly. No one here would ever believe the truth. But the baseness of the lies that had been fabricated against her had left her feeling sick and angry.

'I regret I can make no assignations with you, Prince Tariq,' she declared in an undertone, as Muhammed and Hussein approached them across the sunlit patio. 'After all, how do you know I am not like this—this woman you speak of? How do you know I would not demand proof of the seriousness of your intentions?'

Tariq was taken aback, she could tell, and before he could think of any suitable rejoinder, Hussein was holding out his hands to them, displaying their pristine cleanliness.

'I think it's time we settled down to some proper lessons, Hussein, don't you?' Ashley remarked tightly, taking her son's hand. 'Come along. Your Uncle Tariq has wasted enough time with us, I am sure. And we do not want Muhammed to give Prince Alain a poor report, do we?'

Her gaze challenged Muhammed's as she made this last statement, and she saw the Arab's eyes move speculatively towards his master's brother. She wondered if he had any idea what Tariq had been saying to her, or whether he imagined she might be flattered by the younger man's attentions. Whatever his inner feelings, his expression was enigmatic, and it was left to Tariq to make an abrupt and tight-lipped withdrawal.

CHAPTER NINE

THE following morning Hussein was dejected and heavy-eyed, and showed little aptitude for learning. He sat at his desk, his dark head propped on one small fist, gazing broodingly into space, and only spoke when Ashley addressed a question to him.

'What is the matter?' she said at last, giving in to a reluctant desire to reassure him. She had intended not to encourage his self-pity, but his forlorn little face wrung her heart.

'He did not come,' said Hussein simply, his lower lip trembling a little. 'Uncle Alain did not come to see me. He has been home for two days, and he has not even sent me a present.'

Ashley forced a smile to lift her lips. 'A present?' she exclaimed, trying to sound reproving. 'Is that all you want—a present? And here I was thinking you had missed your Uncle Alain's company.'

'I have! I did!' Hussein was indignant. 'I do not care about a present, not really. I only meant—he has not even thought of me.'

'I'm sure you're mistaken,' said Ashley flatly, acknowledging Alain's importance in Hussein's small world with a sinking heart. 'This trip to America your uncle has taken was on behalf of the government, and naturally his first allegiance must be to them.'

'Al—al—algence?' Hussein was finding it difficult to get his tongue round the word. 'What is that?'

'Allegiance,' repeated Ashley gently. 'It means he has to report to them first. To give them the information for which he was sent.' She sighed. 'I'm sure he's not neglecting you deliberately, darling.' She paused, and then added unwillingly: 'Your uncle isn't like that.'

'Am I not?'

The harsh masculine tones interrupted their exchange with wry mockery, and Ashley's startled response was drowned beneath Hussein's sudden whoop of excitement.

'Uncle Alain!' he squealed, bounding off his chair and across the room, and Alain caught him up in his strong arms and let Hussein wrap himself eagerly about him.

Ashley got to her feet less enthusiastically, struggling to contain her own violent reactions to Alain's appearance. He stood there, tall and dark and disturbingly attractive, in his sleek European clothes, and all the frustration she had suffered at Tariq's hands welled up inside her like a vile-tasting sickness. When he looked at her across Hussein's head, she could hardly prevent the words of accusation from spilling from her lips, and she twisted her hands together painfully, digging her nails into her palms.

'*Eh bien*, little one, and how are the lessons with Mademoiselle progressing?' Alain enquired, drawing his vaguely speculative gaze from Ashley and looking at the boy in his arms with kindly insistence. 'What is all this talk about my neglecting you? Did Miss—Conway not tell you how tied up I have been?'

'Hussein has been rather upset that you haven't been to see him,' Ashley put in tautly, before he could say more. 'I—I explained that if you had had the time, he would have been first on your list.'

Alain's blue eyes narrowed. 'I see,' he said slowly, and she knew he had interpreted her words correctly. 'So you think I should have come to see you before this, eh, little one?' He smiled. 'Then I offer my apologies.'

Ashley would not have believed this, had she not been seeing it with her own eyes. Alain's tenderness with her son was so unexpected, and so natural, and in spite of her resentment she could not doubt his sincerity.

'Did you have a good trip, Uncle Alain?' Hussein was asking excitedly. 'Did you miss me? Did you bring me something back from New York?'

'Hussein!'

Ashley's remonstrance was automatic, but Alain did

not seem put out by the boy's impulsive chatter. On the contrary, setting Hussein down, he felt about his pockets, and while the boy watched in eager anticipation he produced a gaily-wrapped package from his jacket.

Hussein tore off the wrapping paper with careless fingers, and once again Ashley's gaze encountered Alain's as he appraised her silent antipathy. She wondered what he was thinking, what interpretation he was putting upon her attitude, and whether he thought she might be jealous of the attention her son was receiving. Did such thoughts cross Alain's mind? Did he give her that much consideration? Or was he merely amusing himself by deliberately vaunting the boy's favour?

The box inside the wrapping paper contained a silver bracelet—a delicately-moulded circlet, with fine links and a square identity disc. Hussein's name had been engraved upon the disc, and he displayed this to Ashley proudly, after giving his uncle an embracing hug.

'Look, look, *mademoiselle*!' he urged delightedly. 'Is it not pretty? My own bracelet with my own name! Did I not tell you my uncle would not forget?'

Ashley forced herself to admire the expensive bauble, but her emotions were tied in knots, and although her hatred still blazed inside her, she had to suppress it for her son's sake. What did it matter what lies had been told of her! Why should she care what these strangers thought? But the fact remained, she did, and what was more, she knew an overwhelming desire to blow this whole charade apart.

Of course, common sense prevailed. To expose herself would be to destroy what little confidence Hussein had invested in her. It was useless now to regret what might have been, had she known the whole truth. The past was more than a turned page, it was a closed book, and to open its leaves was to court disaster.

'I wondered if you might like to come riding with me,' Alain was saying now, helping Hussein to put on the silver bracelet, and the boy's eyes glowed excitedly.

'Do you mean it? Do you really mean it? Now! At this minute?' He skipped delightedly. 'Oh, yes, yes, please!'

'But what about Miss Conway?' remarked Alain thoughtfully, looking at Ashley again. 'Do you not think she deserves some consideration? After all, you are in the middle of a lesson, are you not?'

Ashley held up her head. 'Naturally, as Hussein has looked forward so much to your coming, I would not dream of preventing him from accompanying you, *monsieur*,' she declared tautly. 'Our lesson can be continued tomorrow, Hussein.' She paused, then added tightly: 'Have fun!'

Hussein grasped Alain's hand then, attempting to drag him towards the door, but his uncle stood firm. 'And what will you do, Miss Conway?' he persisted. 'Does the idea of riding not appeal to you, too?'

Ashley caught her breath. 'You are joking, *monsieur*.'

'No, I am not.' Alain was evidently serious, and now it was Hussein's turn to protest.

'Uncle Alain! Uncle Alain! We are wasting time.' He flicked a careless glance at his teacher. 'Oh, Miss Conway does not want to go riding. Riding is for *men*! You told me so yourself.'

'Ah, but you forget, little one, in Miss Conway's country, women are regarded as equals, *non*?' Alain's expression grew faintly mocking. 'Is that not so, Miss Conway? In England, women often—how do you say it?—wear the trousers?'

'But Grandmama wears trousers,' exclaimed Hussein impatiently, tugging at his sleeve. 'Uncle Alain, come on! Come and help me change into my riding breeches.'

'In a moment,' said his uncle with crisp asperity, and Hussein, sensing the reproof, hung his head a little sulkily. It was obvious he had no wish for anyone to accompany them, and Ashley quickly made her own refusal.

'I have work to do, *monsieur*,' she said, indicating the desk behind her. 'I—there are sums to mark and lessons to prepare——'

'But these things could equally well be attended to later,' Alain retorted, and there was an edge she didn't quite understand to his voice now. 'Come, you can ride, can you not? You are not afraid of horses, are you?'

Ashley sighed. 'I have had a little experience, yes,' she admitted, blessing those occasions she had ridden Lucy's mare. 'But really, *monsieur*——'

'Muhammed!' Alain summoned the silent Arab, waiting outside on the patio. 'Escort Miss Conway to her apartments, if you will, and wait while she changes into more suitable clothes. Hussein and I will wait for you at the stables in fifteen minutes, Miss Conway. Please—do not disappoint us.'

Ashley's indignation was completely overridden. No matter what protest she offered, Alain had an answer for her, and while she could refuse to join them outright, she was very much afraid that if she did so, Alain would not go either. It was an impossible position, and in spite of Hussein's hostility to the idea, she had to accept.

She had no proper rding clothes, of course, but a pair of dark green corded slacks would suffice, and she teamed them with a matching shirt of emerald green silk. Its tied collar and long full sleeves were enveloping, she thought, and unlikely to cause offence to their escort, but she did take a silk scarf with her, too, in order to control the errant waywardness of her hair.

Hussein looked at her in some surprise when she joined him and his uncle at the stables some twenty minutes later. It was the first time he had seen her wearing anything other than dresses, and his green eyes widened in reluctant admiration.

'Are these the kind of trousers of which you were speaking, Uncle Alain?' he enquired, making Ashley overwhelmingly conscious of their revealing contours, and she scarcely understood the sudden darkness in her brother-in-law's eyes.

'Perhaps,' he commented, non-committally, gesturing Muhammed to hold the chestnut mare he had chosen for Ashley to ride. 'But the expression is of only theoretical value, little one, and Miss Conway's clothes are not meant to be a reflection of the role she has chosen.'

Hussein looked puzzled by so many long words, but for once his uncle did not explain. Instead he propelled the boy up on to the back of a gallant little pony, and swung himself into the saddle of a glossy black stallion.

The two Afghan hounds gambolled excitedly about them as they cantered out of the stable yard. Ashley had no trouble in controlling her mare, whose name, Muhammed informed her, was Medina, but she glanced round rather apprehensively at their *burnous*-clad escort, and wondered a trifle anxiously whether she had not over-estimated her own prowess.

It was the first time she had been beyond the walls of the palace, except in the car with Princess Hélène, and that was not the same. Then, the chauffeur had taken the road into Khadesh that she had travelled on the night of her arrival, whereas now she could see the unspoilt beauty of the ocean. It was there, only a few hundred yards distant, blue-green and translucent, and she felt a little regretful when they turned away from its rugged shoreline.

Beyond a group of palm trees, the desert rolled away to the remote reaches of the mountain range. It looked flat and featureless to Ashley, a barren expanse beaten down by the sun's relentless glare, but after only a short distance she looked back to find the sea had dropped from view. It was startling and unnerving, and not a little frightening to realise how quickly one could lose one's bearings, and she wondered with some apprehension how anyone could find their way back without any apparent point of direction. As she rode beside Muhammed, her feelings must have been quite evident, for reaching across to grasp her bridle, he said gently:

'Prince Alain is as familiar with this area as the mountain lion who steals my brother's goats. Do not be alarmed, *mademoiselle*. We will not get lost.'

Ashley managed a small smile in gratitude for Muhammed's understanding, and endeavoured to look about her with more enthusiasm. She was glad she had brought the scarf for her hair, but although the sun was hot, it was not unpleasantly so. Hussein had told her that already the summer heat was fading, and although it was still hot to Ashley, used to cooler northern climes, she had quickly become accustomed to the change of tempera-

ture. And moving, as they were now, there was the wind
to cool her skin and thread its fingers through her loosening hair.

The horses kept to a steady pace, cantering easily over
the hard-packed surface, and Ashley had no trouble in
keeping up with them. Indeed, she began to enjoy the
solid rhythm of the horse beneath her, and had no objec-
tions when the pace quickened to something between a
canter and a gallop. It was exhilarating, and she forgot
for a while all the problems that awaited her back at the
palace. It was only when Alain wheeled his mount and
came back to join her and Muhammed that she was
forced to remember exactly why she was here.

'I wish to speak with Miss Conway,' declared Alain
evenly, insinuating his mount between hers and the tall
Arab's. 'You will ride with Prince Hussein for a while,
Muhammed. See to it that he does not take unnecessary
risks.'

'Said!'

Muhammed bowed his head politely, and rode ahead
to join the boy, who was looking over his shoulder with
some resentment, and Ashley schooled her features again
and avoided the inevitable pitfalls of looking Alain's way.

They rode in silence for some distance, and Ashley's
nerves stretched. For God's sake, why didn't he get on
with it, whatever it was? she fretted inwardly, but out-
wardly she managed to appear composed.

'There are matters which I must discuss with you,' said
Alain at last, in tones that only she could hear, 'but first
I want you to tell me why you looked at me with such—
contempt, in the schoolroom less than an hour ago.'

Ashley sucked in her breath. 'I thought we had finished
with all that, *monsieur*. As—as I recall it, when you left my
apartments two nights ago, you had no further use for
emotional relationships. So why should I satisfy your curiosity now, when my feelings can be of little or no interest
to you?'

'Stop playing with words, Ashley!' Alain's voice was
strained, and he glanced round impatiently to assure
himself that they could not be overheard. 'What hap-

pened the other evening—was not of my choosing. But you are a beautiful woman, as you very well know, and I, as a man, am not unconscious of that fact.'

Ashley licked her lips. 'Am I supposed to be flattered?'

Alain inhaled deeply. 'Ashley, in the name of heaven, stop tormenting me! Do you think I am proud of the fact that you still have the power to stir my emotions, even after what happened? Dear God, it is like a sickness in my blood, but one which I am determined shall not weaken me again!'

'Then why should it matter to you how I look at you?' countered Ashley, gripping the mare's rein with hands that were not quite steady. '*Monsieur*, I find this conversation boring. Perhaps you should come to the point of what you have to say, instead of labouring over imagined insults!'

Alain's eyes glittered. 'I think the imagined insults are yours, not mine,' he snapped. 'But very well. Let us discuss what I have to say first. Then perhaps we can return to this other matter.' He expelled his breath heavily. 'What did my mother tell you of my trip to New York?'

Ashley was briefly speechless. She had expected a discussion concerning Hussein and his schooling, and this unexpected turn of the conversation had taken her by surprise.

'Yes, New York,' repeated Alain harshly. 'You threw your feelings at me the other evening, when I was unprepared for them. I want to know what it was my mother said to you to make you imagine I had done anything to undermine your position here.'

Ashley moved her shoulders wearily. The things she had learned since that night had assumed such proportions in her eyes that she had almost forgotten her reactions to Alain's proposed appointment. But it all came back to her now, in painful detail, and she turned to look at him with accusing eyes.

'Princess Hélène explained how delighted she was at the success you had had in New York,' she stated coldly. 'She even toasted your achievement, albeit in fruit cup.' She held up her head. 'She also explained that as

Murad's representative to the United States, you would necessarily be spending more time there in future, and apart from the small consideration that Hussein will miss you—miss you dreadfully—your father is unlikely to extend my employment, when you are not here to support me!'

Alain bowed his head in silent consideration. Then, lifting it again, he said: 'So you believe you have my support?'

Ashley's colour deepened. 'I believe—I believe you would not dismiss me without cause.'

'So you think I am an honourable man?'

Ashley bent her head. 'In some things,' she muttered unwillingly.

'And my father?'

'Your father doesn't want me here!' declared Ashley tremulously. 'You know he doesn't. He dislikes me. He disapproves of me. He blames me for Hassan's death!' She sighed. 'You're our only hope.'

'Our?'

'Hussein's and mine.'

'So, you wish to stay here?'

'I wish to stay with Hussein,' she corrected him tautly.

'Then relax.' He spoke flatly. 'I shall not be living in New York. I have already told the minister I cannot accept.'

Ashley gasped. 'But—your mother——'

'My father also. Regrettably, they do not understand, I am needed here.'

Ashley could only stare at him. 'But isn't that foolish?'

'You wish me to go?'

'No.' She shook her head, trying to assimilate this new situation. 'Alain——'

'I also appreciate my responsibilities,' he interrupted her roughly. 'I know that Hussein depends on me. And I—shall not betray the trust he places in me.'

Ashley pressed her lips together. 'Even though you deny him his birthright!'

'Do not say that!'

'Why not? Do you think if I hadn't been certain of the truth I would have let you take him?'

'Enough!' His face was taut and driven. 'You will not say these things to me. Is it not enough that I have taken the child, brought him up in his father's house, given him everything that money can buy? Do not taunt me with his conception, I beg of you. Believe me, I too have suffered enough!'

'You!' Ashley's voice rose on a sob, as emotion tore into her. 'You have suffered!' she repeated half hysterically, and the mare shifted restlessly at the disruptive sound. 'How dare you say it? How can you mouth such things to me! My God, you're a hypocrite, Alain, after the lies you've told to protect yourself!'

'A hypocrite? I am no hypocrite!' Alain's horse swerved as his hands tightened convulsively on the reins. The black stallion snorted in protest, bringing its proud head closer to the mare's neck, and Medina whinnied plaintively as Alain's boot pressed Ashley's knee into the mare's side. 'What fairy story is this you have dreamed up, to justify your own mistakes?'

'It's no fairy story,' retorted Ashley hotly, glad that Muhammed and Hussein were some yards ahead of them, and out of hearing of their exchange. 'Tariq told me—your own brother. He happened to be discussing the unhappy instance of Hussein's birth.'

'With you?' Alain's blue eyes were steely, and Ashley nodded.

'Oh, don't worry, it was all perfectly objective. He just mentioned that Hassan's wife had been well paid for her participation in Hussein's adoption by his father's family.'

Alain's mouth hardened. 'Then he had no right to do so.'

'Why not? It's what he believes.'

'It is what my father has told him,' contradicted Alain grimly.

Ashley was sceptical. 'Not you?'

'Of course not. I would not lie about something like that.'

'Yet you did lie about our relationship, didn't you?' Ashley pressed, pushing the mare dangerously closer, so that both horses shied in protest. 'No wonder you were not surprised when Hassan turned up in London. He came at your instigation, didn't he? To extricate you from your unfortunate involvement with a silly little English student!'

Alain was having difficulty in controlling his horse, but at her words he turned to stare at her incredulously. It was then that the black stallion reared, its highly-strung temperament objecting most strongly to such careless treatment, and while Alain hung on for grim death, the little mare took off at a panic-stricken gallop. Ashley clung to its back with terrified hands, scarcely aware of Hussein's frightened face as she raced past him and Muhammed, intent only on staying with the animal and not being catapulted into the sand.

But it was an unequal battle. She was unused to riding, and already the insides of her legs felt chafed and raw, her fingers cramped around the leader strap of the reins. Although she lay low across the saddle, reducing the buffeting force of the wind, she was rapidly losing her grip, and the sudden appearance of Alain alongside her, reaching determinedly for the mare's bridle, came too late to save her. As he tugged forcefully at the bit, bringing the sweating mare to a halt, Ashley slid helplessly to the ground. Her lungs were winded by the abrupt dismounting, and the sand proved amazingly hard to her throbbing head, and she lay there for several seconds with her eyes closed and panting before a muscular arm was thrust beneath her shoulders.

'Ashley, are you hurt?' Alain's husky voice demanded savagely. 'I am sorry, it was my fault. I could not keep Youssef in control, and I will never forgive myself if I have hurt you!'

Ashley's eyes flickered open at his words, and she was scarcely conscious of her injuries as she gazed up into those disturbed blue irises. Alain was leaning over her anxiously, his white shirt unbuttoned, his chest rising and falling rapidly with the urgency of his distress. His arm was around her, the moist heat of his body mingling with the scent of some shaving lotion he was wearing, and his concern was unmistakable as he smoothed the damp hair back from her forehead.

'I—I'm all right, Alain,' she breathed unevenly, putting up a hand to touch him, scarcely aware of what she was doing in the emotive fever of the moment. Her fingertips probed the faint scars that still lingered where she had put her mark upon him, then dropped lower to trail sensuously over the lightly-matted hair on his chest.

'Are you sure?' he demanded huskily, running an exploring hand over her shoulder and down the silk-clad length of her arm. 'That does not hurt you does it? There are no bones broken? For God, Ashley, when you dashed away like that, I almost lost my reason!'

Ashley expelled her breath unsteadily. 'Why?' she whispered, 'why should it matter to you, Alain?'

'Because, God help me, it does!' he grated harshly, and before she could define his intentions he gathered her closer and pressed his hard mouth against hers.

Ashley's lips parted involuntarily. She was still not sufficiently recovered from the shock of falling to offer any resistance, and besides, beneath that brief but passionate caress, her senses swam without heed. His lips against hers made an intimacy of his assault on her emotions, and her hand sought his nape instinctively, as she responded without hesitation to the hunger of his kiss.

The thunder of hooves as the rest of the party cantered up to them seemed to bring Alain to his senses. With an expression almost of revulsion, Ashley felt, crossing his lean tanned face, he dragged himself away from her, assisting her to her feet with the casual pressure of his hand.

'What is wrong? What has happened?' Hussein swung down from his pony beside them, gazing at Ashley with a faint look of accusation. 'Are you ill, *mademoiselle*? Did Medina run away with you?' He looked up at his uncle and pursed his small lips. 'What were you doing, bending over her so closely?'

Alain drew a steadying breath, and Ashley swayed a

little as he released her arm. 'Miss Conway's mare bolted, Hussein,' he replied, as Muhammed dismounted also and came towards them. 'Will you take Miss Conway back to the palace, Muhammed? I fear she is not strong enough to continue on to Numara.'

Muhammed bowed his head in acquiescence, and even Hussein looked mollified by this news. But Ashley was curiously loath to be despatched back to the palace like a unwanted parcel, and pushing back the tumbled weight of her hair, she put her hand on Alain's sleeve.

'Really,' she said, feeling the hard muscle beneath the fine silk, 'I'm all right, Alain, honestly.'

She realised her mistake the moment Hussein sucked in his breath. In spite of his growing attachment to her, she was still only the governess, and to hear her using his uncle's Christian name seemed worthy of castigation in his childish eyes. With an open mouth displaying his outrage, he watched his uncle with bated breath, and Ashley, realising she had made the error, hastily tried to redeem her mistake.

'Oh, I'm sorry,' she burst out hurriedly, withdrawing her hand in some confusion. 'Prince Alain, you must forgive me. I—I don't know what came over me. I think I must still be a little dizzy after falling from the horse.'

Hussein's mouth closed, but his sense of indignation remained, and it was left to Alain to restore the status quo. 'It is completely understandable,' he said, his voice taut and unnatural. 'And I think you must agree that it would be—safer to return to the palace. Muhammed will escort you, and I trust you will feel better soon.'

'I'm sure I shall.' Ashley spoke a little stiffly now, her blood cooling to leave the disturbing weight of what had happened bearing down upon her. 'Thank—thank you for your concern, Prince Alain.'

Alain turned abruptly away from her, as if he could not bear to go on looking at her, and putting his hands on Hussein's waist he swung the boy back up on to his pony.

'Until later, Muhammed,' he muttered, in an undertone, mounting the black stallion, and Ashley watched with a dry mouth as her son and the man he regarded as his uncle rode off into the shimmering haze.

'May I help you, *mademoiselle*?' Muhammed's respectful voice aroused her from he dark depths of her reveriend with a faint movement of her shoulders she nodded her head.

'The boy meant no harm, *mademoiselle*,' Muhammed added, as she placed her foot in his cupped hands, and she realised he had interpreted her dejection as a symptom of her hopeless love for Hussein. If only it was that simple, she thought, giving the tall Arab a grateful smile. If only Hussein's love was all she craved . . .

CHAPTER TEN

THE day dragged interminably by. Aching in every limb from the unaccustomed exercise, Ashley waited tautly for the summons she was sure would come, but as the evening shadows lengthened, she conceded that Alain did not plan to discharge her tonight. Instead she allowed Nuzab to coax her into taking a bath, and before dinner was served she relaxed in the scented water the Arab girl had prepared for her. It was an unwilling indulgence, but Ashley's tormented emotions were salved by Nuzab's gentle massage, and she gave herself up to the unthinking, unfeeling numbness of inertia.

By the time her skin had been soaped and dried and scented with sandalwood, Ashley was feeling infinitely more optimistic. With the honey-gold curtain of her hair loose about her shoulders, she left Nuzab to empty the tub, and walked into her bedroom wrapping the cream silk robe Princess Hélène had given her about her slim body. There was no point in dressing again, she had decided. She would eat a little of the dinner Nuzab would serve, and then go to bed. Maybe Alain would send for her in the morning, or maybe he would not. Either way, there was no point in flaying herself unnecessarily.

Concentrating on tying the cord of her gown, she did not immediately notice the man who was standing in the open doorway that led from the salon into her bedroom, but when she did, she started abruptly, one hand going automatically to draw together the wrapover neckline of the robe.

'Alain!' she exclaimed, and then more composedly: '*Prince* Alain! Wh-what are you doing here? I—I thought you would be with your father by now.'

Alain watched her silently, his eyes brooding. It was an unnerving appraisal, worthy of Prince Ahmed at his most intimidating, and Ashley had to sustain that stare when she was unprepared and unarmed, and at her most vulnerable. It was not his attire that intimidated her. This evening he was wearing European clothes, and the dark brown velvet trousers that moulded the powerful length of his legs, and the full-sleeved silk shirt, accentuated his French ancestry rather than his Arab blood. But the expression in his cold blue eyes was totally alien, and she waited with real apprehension for the anger that was to come.

'Where is Nuzab?' he asked at last, straightening from his indolent stance and looking briefly beyond her, as if in enquiry.

'She—she's emptying the bath,' replied Ashley tautly, tightening the cord of her robe almost symbolically. 'I—er—won't you go through to the salon? I'm sure we could talk more easily in there.'

Alain hesitated, and as he did so, Nuzab appeared behind Ashley. She bowed low when she saw her mistress's visitor, then waited impassively for her instructions.

'I shall be dining with Miss Conway this evening, Nuzab,' Alain announced coolly, much to Ashley's indignation. 'You may bring the food when you are ready. We will serve ourselves.'

'Yes, *Said*.'

Nuzab bowed again as she made her departure, and Ashley, on the point of countering his orders, bit her tongue. What was the use of arguing with him? He would always have his way here. And how could she use Nuzab as a weapon, when the Arab girl might only suffer later? She had grown attached to her dark-skinned companion, and she would not like Nuzab to be punished because of her.

Left alone with Alain, Ashley squared her shoulders. 'As it appears you intend to stay for some time, *monsieur*, perhaps you would permit me to put on some clothes. I didn't expect any visitors this evening, and as you can see, my toilette is not complete.'

'I like what you are wearing,' retorted Alain, without

expression. 'Come, we will do as you suggested and go into the salon. Nuzab will serve dinner there, and we have plenty of time.'

Ashley didn't quite understand what he meant by this, but deciding not to provoke any unpleasantness, she walked past him into the room beyond. He stood aside to allow her progress, and the heat of his skin seemed to reach out and envelop her. The smell of his body disturbed her; it was out of keeping with his cool exterior. But she seated herself with apparent calmness on a low couch, and wrapped her skirts about her bare legs.

'I—I suppose you've come about—about what happened this morning,' she began, speaking quickly because her nerves would not allow much more of this game of cat and mouse. 'I—I know I was careless. I know I made a mistake. But—but surely anyone—anyone can do that?'

Alain came to stand some distance from her, his arms folded across his flat stomach, his booted feet stationed some inches apart. 'How are you feeling?' he asked, without answering her, and taking an unsteady breath, Ashley assured him that she was fine.

'I—I was a little stiff, that's all,' she explained. 'But—but I took a bath, and I'm feeling much—much better.'

'Good.' Alain inclined his head. 'It could have been more serious. Fortunately, Medina was scarcely moving when you slipped from her back.'

'Yes,' Ashley nodded. 'I—I have you to thank for that.'

Alain made no response to this statement, but his hands fell to his sides, and he moved restlessly across the room. 'Nuzab takes her time,' he remarked grimly. 'How long does it take to wheel a trolley along a corridor?'

'She's only been gone a few minutes,' Ashley demurred, stung by his impatience. Was he so eager to escape from the contamination of her presence? she wondered. And if so, why had he chosen to join her in the first place?

She wished he would sit down. His pacing was almost as bad as his brooding assessment had been. What was he doing here? Why had he come? Why couldn't he tell her, instead of keeping her in this awful state of suspense?

Tilting her head, she looked up at him determinedly, and squeezing all her small store of confidence together, she said: 'Why don't you tell me why you've really come here, Prince Alain?'

Her words halted him at least, and he turned to look at her with a piercing blue gaze. 'Have done with calling me Prince Alain,' he snapped harshly. 'You do not think of me that way, any more than I think of you as Miss Conway, or Miss Gilbert either, for that matter.' His mouth compressed. 'We will wait until Nuzab has brought the food. I have no intention of discussing my affairs within the hearing of such sharp little ears.'

Ashley sighed, and bent her head. 'But if you're going to find some reason to dismiss me, isn't she going to find out sooner or later?' she asked dully, and started violently when he covered the space between them with almost threatening speed.

'Did I say I was going to dismiss you?' he demanded, his hand reaching out almost against his will, and twining convulsively in her hair. 'So soft!' he muttered. 'So silky!' He bent his head and pressed his face to a handful, only to step back jerkily when the heavy doors were suddenly propelled open.

If Nuzab saw anything unusual in the fact that her master's son was standing suspiciously close to the young English governess's couch, or observed that the fine silk fall of hair she herself had brushed was now a little dishevelled, she knew better than to reveal her reactions. Working diligently, she quickly laid a marble-topped table with silver dishes and silver cutlery, and left the various courses simmering above their tiny gas flames. Although the room was lit by lamps, she lighted two candles and set them on the table, and then offered her work for Ashley's inspection, smiling shyly when she was complimented on her skill.

'I will come back later to clear the dishes, lady,' she said, but here again Alain intervened.

'Miss Conway will summon you, if she needs your assistance,' he declared, speaking with more brusqueness than was usual to the bowing Nuzab. 'Go! Make yourself scarce. Your services will not be required tonight.'

Nuzab looked at Ashley, but she could only shake her head. Her own reactions to Alain's words were too chaotic to extricate, and as soon as the Arab girl had left them she turned on her tormentor.

'Did you have to do that?' she demanded tautly. 'Did you have to behave as if I was some kind of concubine with whom you intended to spend the night? For God's sake, you know what the servants are like, Alain! What are you trying to do? Get your father to dismiss me on grounds of promiscuity?'

Alain's eyes had narrowed in the course of her dissertation, and she trembled violently when he came to stand in front of her. 'Would that be so bad?' he murmured, rubbing the palm of one hand insistently over the silky robe on her shoulder. 'Spending the night with me, I mean? Does that sound so objectionable to you?'

Ashley caught her breath and whirled away from him, putting half a dozen paces between them before she trusted herself to speak. 'Is that what all this is about?' she choked disbelievingly. 'Is that what this elaborate charade is intended to achieve? An opportunity for you to spend the night with me, Alain?' She gasped. 'My God! And I thought you were going to fire me!'

'There is no need for you to become hysterical, Ashley,' Alain retorted tightly, the tip of his tongue moistening his lips. 'It is what you have wanted—what we *both* have wanted—and I see no reason to deny us something so elemental.'

'You don't see any reason!' Ashley swallowed convulsively. 'God in Heaven! You have a nerve!'

'Why? Why do I have a nerve?' he asked insistently, moving irresistibly towards her. 'Was it not always this way between us? Was it not always impossible to control?'

'No! *No!*' Ashley backed away from him nervously, and then, realising she was behaving foolishly, she forced herself to stand still. 'I—I learned from—from Tariq exactly how—how controllable your feelings were, Alain, and—and I have no intention of allowing you to hurt me again!'

'I? Hurt you?' he enquired, with some incredulity. 'Oh, Ashley, that was never the way.' With careful indulgence he stroked the errant strands of hair back from her ears, and then bent his head to explore their hollows with his tongue. 'You were not hurt, only thwarted,' he whispered huskily, and she dragged herself back from him and raised her fists.

'I think not,' said Alain dryly, capturing her hands before they could reach their target. 'You have no idea how embarrassing it was, having to explain that I scratched my face on a rose bush. I want no further injuries to expose my weaknessses, even though I doubt your puny strength could achieve so much.'

Ashley's lips trembled. 'Why are you doing this, Alain? Why? You don't really want me. You don't. You just want to humiliate me, to show me you can still make a fool of me. Oh, for pity's sake, let me go, let me go! I—I can't bear it when you treat me like a—a discarded possession!'

'But you are not a discarded possession, Ashley, are you?' Alain demanded harshly, releasing her wrists to put his hands on her waist. Through the fine silk, their strength and hardness was unmistakable, and Ashley wondered if he was aware that she was naked beneath the robe. 'I did not discard you,' he continued, glittering blue eyes boring into hers. 'You discarded me—for Hassan. Or had you forgotten?'

'That's not true!' Ashley drew an unsteady breath. 'Alain, I've told you—a dozen times. Hassan meant nothing to me, nothing! Until you abandoned me, and I used him to get back at you.'

'So you admit it!' Alain's face was grim, and his hands at her waist had tightened painfully. 'You admit that you *used* my brother. That you were the instrument of his death!'

'No!' Ashley's eyes were wide. 'You know how Hassan died. He killed himself—he deliberately drove his car into a tree. And you know why he did it, too, if you would only listen to your brain and not your emotions!'

Alain took several deep breaths, evidently trying to keep those same emotions in check. The conversation was not going the way he had intended, and she guessed he had not bargained for her unqualified resistance.

'I did not come here to discuss Hassan's untimely end,' he said at last, his hands relaxing their grip, even while he propelled her closer. 'I came because you are still like a fever in my blood, and in spite of my distrust of you, I still find your body irresistible.'

Ashley's palms pressed against his chest, holding him off, but only so long as it suited him to allow her to do so. 'And—and you think you can come here and make love to me any time you feel like it, is that it?' she choked, wishing she could hate him for his arrogance, yet still ignominiously drawn to his dark masculinity.

'I did not say anything about—making love,' he corrected her huskily. 'I said I wanted your body, and I do. I want to see your beautifully corrupt form laid out for my delectation, and I want to feel that silken sheath around me. But I said nothing about love, Ashley. Making love has nothing to do with it!'

Ashley's features felt frozen in an attitude of numbed mortification, but although her response to his scornful denunciation was one of desperation, she knew she would never defeat him by angry resentment or reasoned debate. Alain was beyond those things. He despised her, and he despised himself for wanting her, but in this instance his will could not prevail. Her only hope of convincing him lay within the bounds of his admitted need of her, and somehow she had to use her body to make him see the truth.

Using what small amount of control she still possessed, Ashley made no move to draw away from him, as she guessed he had expected, judging by the tightening grip of his fingers, and instead allowed one pearl-tipped finger nail to probe the buttoned fastening of his shirt. 'Tell me, Alain,' she murmured, feeling his unwilling stiffening beneath her touch, 'why do you think I—gave myself to Hassan? What do you think he had, that you had not?'

Alain's breathing was hoarse. 'What kind of a question is that?' he grated, his arms sliding round her waist, compelling her against him.

'A valid one, surely,' Ashley persisted, still resisting him, although the tautness of his thighs was unmistakable through the silken folds of her gown. 'Alain, have you never wondered when Hassan and I had time to get to know one another so intimately? I spent all my free time with you. I hardly knew your brother!'

'You married him,' retorted Alain harshly, his face close to hers, his eyes frankly sensuous. 'Let us have done with this foolishness, Ashley. I am growing impatient. I do not want to force you, but if I have to, I will.'

'You've never forced me before,' she reminded him, quivering in spite of her determination to remain calm when his tongue found the corner of her lips. 'Alain, listen to me, please! Listen to me! How can you believe I could let Hassan touch me, when you had only to be near me to make me want to be with you?'

'I do not want to talk about Hassan!' declared Alain savagely. 'In God's name, Ashley, let the past die. How can you even speak of your husband when I am holding you like this? What are you trying to do—make me feel guilty?'

'No.' Ashley had to be honest, but Alain's eyes had a growing accusation in their depths. 'I'm only trying to defend myself, can't you see? I'm trying to convince you that you're the only man who has ever been a part of me!'

'*Nom de Dieu!*' With a groan of anguish, Alain thrust her away from him then, pushing unsteady fingers through the thickness of his hair, turning aside from her with bitter determination. 'All right, all right,' he muttered, closing his eyes. 'You win. I will not touch you. But as God is my witness, you deserve my contempt!'

Ashley trembled uncontrollably. This was not what she had wanted at all. On the contrary, she wanted Alain so weak with longing for her that he had no choice but to take her, and with a little cry she went after him, winding her arms around his waist from behind.

'You don't understand, you don't understand!' she cried, pressing herself against him, feeling the shudder that went through his body at her touch. 'Alain, Alain, don't go; don't go, please! I want to talk that's all. Talk, damn you! Oh, Alain, Alain, don't leave me!'

His hands had gone to his waist, to extricate himself from her binding arms, but somehow it didn't work out the way he planned it. Instead of wrenching himself away, he turned to face her, and the tearful reproach in her eyes destroyed the barriers he would have erected. With a sensual twisting of his mouth, he reached almost compulsively to the cord at her waist, pulling it free so that the two sides swung apart. Then he jerked her against him, her slim naked body free and unconfined in his arms, as he bent his head to take her lips.

The urgent pressure of his mouth was a potent provocation, and her lips opened eagerly to him. Her senses swam beneath his eager conquest, and acting purely on instinct she pressed herself against him. She wanted to extend that intimate embrace, to feel his skin warm against hers, and when his hands tore his shirt from his pants, her hands rushed to help him. The buttons were ripped from their holes, and one or two spilled on to the floor in his haste, but then the fine cloud of body hair that arrowed down to his navel was cushioning her breasts, crushing them closer to the tautly-muscled width of his chest.

Panic briefly flared inside her as he swung her up into his arms and carried her across the salon and into her bedroom. What was she doing? she asked herself wildly, looking up into his dark driven face. What manner of retribution could she expect, if Alain chose to punish her for this? It was not the way he had planned it, this she knew, and his uncontrollable need for her was more than the physical appeasement he had spoken of. When he kissed her, when he held her in his arms, the emotions he was feeling were unmistakable, and although she was exhilarated that this should be so, she was unsure of her ability to sustain them.

He had left her once before. He had spurned her and left her in the jealous hands of his brother. He might well do it again, and this time he would ensure there would be no reconciliation.

She shifted anxiously in his arms, but it was too late now for such misgivings. In any case, when he laid her on the bed and seconds later joined her, she was too bemused by the warm pressure of his body to make any protest.

Besides, she wanted him; it was that simple. She wanted him so desperately she was amazed she had lived so long without the hungry possession of his body, and the urgent passion in his eyes was just a reflection of her own.

'You are so beautiful,' he groaned, his long fingers cupping her breasts. 'Oh, Ashley, you do not want to deny me, do you? You want this as much as I do.'

'In cold blood,' she managed huskily, as his lips trailed a fiery path down to her navel, and he raised his head to look at her with burning eyes.

'Is that what you think?' he demanded, as her fingers slid through his hair, and her breathing quickened at his sudden anger.

'It's what you said,' she reminded him softly, and he slid over her urgently, seeking her lips with his.

'How could you believe me?' he muttered, against her mouth. 'Do you not know what you do to me, what you have always done to me? Dear God, Ashley, it was always love between us. That was what made it all so painful!'

'Was it painful for you?' she persisted, as his tongue played with her lips, and she felt the shuddering revulsion that ran over him at her words.

'I wanted to kill you,' he admitted in a muffled voice, his face buried in the silken curtain of her hair. 'And because I could not do that, I resolved to hurt you, in any way I could.'

'Like—like taking our son from me,' Ashley suggested in a breathless voice, and Alain raised himself on his elbows to look down into her sensually flushed, yet troubled, features.

'You persist in this calumny,' he protested, with harsh impatience. 'Ashley, is it not enough that I have admitted my need for you? Must you continually remind me of your betrayal?'

'There was no betrayal, Alain,' she insisted, lifting her slim arms to wind them around his neck, and he was not immune to their silken embrace. With a groan of submission he allowed her to draw him down to her, and her next words were spoken against his cheek.

'Think of it, Alain,' she breathed, arching herself against him. 'Hussein is *your* son—yours and mine! We made him, you and I. Don't you think he's like you? Don't you see he resembles you?'

'No——' Alain's denial was hoarse, but Ashley was determined.

'He *is* like you. Exactly like you. Why do you think I let you take him? If he had been Hassan's son, do you think I would have given him away so easily? No! No! It was because he was yours, yours! And I knew you could give him a better start in life than I ever could.'

'*No!*'

Alain was incensed, but Ashley knew she had sown the first real seeds of doubt in his mind. It was there in the rapid darkening of his eyes, in the mobile anger in his mouth, and in the sudden violence with which he took her. He wanted to shut her up, to silence her, to show her he was still the master of the situation. But instead, after that initial invasion of her body, his fury dissipated in the passionate evocation of their lovemaking.

Ashley gasped at the thrusting fire of his possession. But the sweet, mindless sensations he quickly aroused inside her sent all coherent thought from her head, and she responded to his savagery with instinctive sensuality, turning his grim determination into an irresistible compulsion and his fury to a wine-dark hunger. He could not sustain his anger, when his hands clung to her body and his mouth fed from her lips, and what began as a bitter assault changed eagerly to a mutual supplication.

Ashley's blood ran like liquid fire through her veins as the feeling he was evoking brought a moan of pleasure to her lips. Her hands caressed his back, running urgently over his moist skin, stroking and caressing and inducing his surrender, until his teeth fastened sensuously into her tormenting flesh. She was like a flame in his arms, twisting beneath him and inciting his emotions, crying out in fulfilment.

The aftermath came with reluctance. Ashley did not want to let him go, and when he stirred with indolent lethargy she wound herself about him and would not let him move away.

'Ashley,' he groaned in protest, lifting his head and brushing the clinging strands of her hair from his lips. 'Ashley, I think you have proved your point, have you not?' His blue eyes were heavy-lidded and glazed with the languorous effects of their union. 'You must know this was not how I intended it to be, but I lose my senses when I am with you, and I almost believe what you say to be true.'

'It is true, *it is*!' exclaimed Ashley urgently, grasping his shoulders, but Alain only shook his head and firmly pulled away.

'You are a witch!' he muttered, after he had extricated himself from her clinging limbs, and was sitting on the side of the bed. 'My God! You almost make me believe that no other man has ever touched you! What is this power you have?' He massaged his neck muscles with some impatience. 'I will not let you humiliate me again!'

Ashley hesitated only a second, then she too got up, making no attempt to cover herself as she stepped in front of him. 'Was that what it was, Alain?' she breathed, her hair falling demurely over her breasts. 'A bewitching? A humiliation?' She spread her hands. 'You must know in your heart Hassan never touched me. He—he tried, but he couldn't. Oh, Alain, listen to me, listen to me—Hassan was impotent!'

Alain's graven features terrified her, and with a whirling movement that sent her hair swirling about her she ran across the room to the bathroom, closing the door and leaning against it, willing him to go while she still had the power to hold back her grief. If he didn't believe her now, he never would, and she couldn't bear to see the destruction of something she had begun to believe in.

The forced opening of the door behind her sent her scurrying into the shower cubicle, and when Alain appeared beside her she gazed at him with wide, wounded eyes.

'Why don't you go?' she demanded, unknowingly desirable in her pathetic defiance, and Alain, who was already partially dressed, gazed at her with sudden frustration.

'Why don't I go?' he muttered, his hands clenching tautly. 'Indeed, why don't I go? That is a good question.' He shook his head bitterly, and took a step towards her. 'Perhaps because, like all fools, I do not know when to give in.'

'I—I'll turn on the water,' she exclaimed threateningly, groping for the gold tap. 'If—if you don't go away——'

'—you will soak us both,' he agreed huskily, and even as her fingers set the shower in motion, he stepped into the cubicle with her.

She shivered convulsively as the cascade of cool water came down upon them, but Alain seemed uncaring of the fact that his velvet trousers were getting wet. With a curiously wry twisting of his expression, he reached for her again, and the falling spray was merely the fusing element that bound their two bodies together ...

CHAPTER ELEVEN

ALAIN was gone when she awakened.

The sound of Nuzab drawing the blinds evoked a momentary panic inside her, as her aching limbs bore witness to Alain's repeated possession, and the memories of the night before flooded back in disturbing detail. But the bed beside her was empty. She was alone, with only the evidence of her nakedness to betray what had happened to the Arab girl.

'*Saida*, lady,' Nuzab greeted her as usual, setting her breakfast tray to one side, when Ashley made no immediate effort to prepare herself to take it. In truth, she was trying to decide how best to explain her lack of attire, but Nuzab, it seemed, had other things on her mind. 'You did not eat any dinner last evening,' she went on, with gentle accusation. 'The food—it was not to yours or my lord's taste? You have some complaint to make?'

Ashley shifted the silken sheet more closely about her shoulders. 'The food—oh, the food!' She forced a faint smile. 'I'm afraid I wasn't hungry, Nuzab.'

'But Prince Alain——'

'Prince Alain—left,' declared Ashley firmly, choosing the easy way out. 'He—he did not eat dinner with me.' That, at least, was true!

Nuzab pursed her lips. 'But where was he, lady?' she asked in some confusion. 'When his father, Prince Ahmed, asked for him, he could not be found.'

Ashley sighed. 'I don't know, do I?' she retorted shortly, wishing the Arab girl would leave her to eat her breakfast in peace, but Nuzab could be annoyingly persistent, as the English girl already knew.

'Is most strange,' she declared, shaking her head so that her long black braids swung over her shoulders.

'Even Muhammed could not find him, and Prince Ahmed was very angry.'

Ashley forced a calmness she was far from feeling. 'But—this morning; he's been found, hasn't he?'

'Yes, lady,' Nuzab nodded. 'He joined his father for the morning meal, and without doubt he will spend the rest of the day with the Princess.'

Ashley wriggled a little higher on her pillows, tucking the sheet sarong-wise under her arms. 'You mean his mother?' she enquired, hoping Nuzab would not notice the slight bruising on her arms as she reached for the tray, but the Arab girl's next words drove all thoughts of modesty out of her head.

'His mother, lady?' she echoed. 'Ah, you think I mean the Princess Hélène.' Nuzab smiled. 'No, it is the Princess Ramira. Did you not know? She and her father, Prince Khalil, arrived last evening.'

Ashley's mouth felt suddenly dry. 'But who is Princess Ramira, Nuzab?' she asked, with sudden apprehension, and the Arab girl smiled in recognition that her news was of interest at last.

'She is the friend of Prince Alain, lady,' she averred, with characteristic fervency. 'They have been friends for many years. I think Prince Ahmed would welcome her as Prince Alain's wife.'

Ashley was washed and dressed when Nuzab returned to take the tray, and the Arab girl looked with some distress at the untouched food.

'But you have not eaten!' she exclaimed, and Ashley avoided her eyes as she applied a brick-coloured gloss to her lips.

'I drank some coffee,' she replied in protest, checking the fastening of the cream cotton smock that successfully disguised the palpitating beat of her heart. 'Don't fuss so, Nuzab. I shall eat when I'm hungry, never fear.'

Nuzab hesitated, looking doubtfully at the tray in her hands. 'Lady is not well?' she suggested. 'Lady have—argument with my master last evening?'

Ashley stroked a concealing brush over her suddenly

flushed cheeks. 'You're imagining things, Nuzab. I've told you what happened. Now please leave me alone.'

The Arab girl sthlh–tood her ground. 'Nuzab think lady let my master upset her,' she declared with some temerity. 'Nuzab know my master spend many hours with—with you.'

Ashley gasped. 'How do you know that?'

'Nuzab come back for trolley,' explained the Arab girl reluctantly. 'My lady not in salon. Nuzab—hear voices.'

Ashley did look at her then, her whole face suffused with colour. 'You mean—you mean you *watched* us!' she demanded huskily, but Nuzab hastily shook her head.

'No! No, lady, Nuzab not do such thing.' Her wounded dark eyes bore witness to her innocence, and Ashley's blood pressure subsided a little.

'But you heard us?' she persisted tautly, and the Arab girl nodded her head. 'What time was this?'

'About—about midnight, lady.'

'Midnight!' Ashley moistened her dry lips. 'So why didn't you say so earlier?'

Nuzab bent her head. 'It is not my business, lady.'

'But now you've made it so.'

'Nuzab worry about lady,' she responded, and Ashley could not sustain her anger in the face of the girl's evident sincerity.

'Well, don't worry, Nuzab,' she said now, getting to her feet and putting a sympathetic hand on the girl's shoulders. 'I'm all right really. I—just need a little time to—to decide what I'm going to do.'

'What to do, lady?' Nuzab looked up at her wide-eyed. 'But you will come now to see Prince Hussein.'

'Oh, yes,' Ashley nodded, 'I'll come to see Prince Hussein now. But—ultimately—I don't know, Nuzab. I just don't know.'

Being with her son was like a salve to her feelings of raw vulnerability. Obviously, Alain must have given Hussein his orders concerning the way he was to behave, and his polite enquiry as to her health, and his hope that she had suffered no ill effects from her fall the previous day, were pure mimicry. Even so, away from Alain's influence, he did show a more sympathetic side to his nature, but she understood only too well how hard it was for him to share Alain's attentions with anyone. Hadn't she once been the same?

While her son struggled to master the arts of multiplication and division, Ashley tried to draw some conclusions from what she had learned. Nuzab's innocent betrayal of the presence of another woman in the palace took on a different aspect when allied to her knowledge of Alain's whereabouts the night before. Had Prince Ahmed really instituted a search for his son, or had it simply been Nuzab's way of showing her how futile it would be to imagine any good could come from getting involved with any of the male members of the Prince's family? Was it really important to know? Or was it not simply a case of the facts speaking for themselves, as they had done so many times in the past?

Running a weary hand over her perspiring temple, Ashley tried to be objective, but it was almost impossible after what had happened the night before. Whatever his motives, Alain had made love to her, and because of this, her position was both strengthened and weakened. Alain wanted her. He could not deny that. But because of this, he might well consider the only solution was to be rid of her, before she created a situation he could not control. Was that why he had brought this woman here? This Princess Ramira, whom Nuzab seemed to think he might marry? Alain had told her categorically that he had no intention of marrying anyone, but he was his father's heir, and as such he had certain responsibilities. What if he decided those responsibilities outweighed any loyalty he owed to his dead brother? For as long as he regarded Hussein as Hassan's son, it was only his brother's memory he was respecting.

Ashley sighed, and Hussein lifted his head enquiringly. 'Are you tired, *mademoiselle*?' he asked, his soft lips parting, and she knew a sudden sense of futility for what she was trying to do. Being Hussein's governess was not going to be enough: Alain had been right about that. Now that the initial thrill of being her son's companion was over, she wanted more from their relationship, much more, more in fact than any governess had any right to expect. But she was his mother! *His mother!* And with every day that passed, the desire to tell him grew stronger and stronger.

Now Ashley forced a smile and shook her head. 'I was just thinking, that's all,' she said, supporting her chin on the slender knuckles of one hand. 'How is the arithmetic going? How many of those sums have you done?'

'Three,' admitted Hussein reluctantly, viewing the seven still to be done without enthusiasm. Then: 'What were you thinking about, *mademoiselle*? Were you thinking of Uncle Tariq?'

'*Tariq?*' The name slipped from Ashley's lips unthinkingly, but fortunately Hussein seemed not to notice. 'No. No, why should you think that? What has your Uncle Tariq to do with me?'

Hussein shrugged. 'He likes you, I know he does.'

'How do you know that?' Ashley flushed.

'Aunt Melina told me,' replied Hussein carelessly. 'You have met my aunt. She was my father's sister.'

Ashley made a helpless gesture. Of course, Melina had been present the evening she dined with Princess Izmay. The evening Tariq had devoted his attentions to her.

'So?' Hussein arched his dark brows. 'You see, we have no secrets in the palace.'

Ashley hid a grimace at the irony of this, but Hussein's next words were more disturbing. 'I told Uncle Alain,' he declared, chewing on his pencil, and now he had his mother's undivided attention.

'What—what did you tell—Uncle Alain?' she ventured apprehensively, and Hussein took the pencil out of his mouth to view her with more intensity.

'You look—odd, *mademoiselle*,' he remarked, his forehead furrowing anxiously, but Ashley only dismissed his concern, and urged him to continue.

'Your uncle,' she prompted, trying to remain calm.

'What did you tell your uncle about—about me?'

'Oh,' Hussein shrugged indifferently, 'I told him what Aunt Melina had said. That Uncle Tariq seemed to like you a lot. That he comes to the schoolroom to see you.'

'Hussein!' Ashley gasped. She could imagine how that would sound to Alain. Then, with sudden comprehension: 'When? When did you tell him this, Hussein? Please—I want to know.'

Hussein was beginning to look sulky now. 'Why? What does it matter?'

'Hussein!'

'Well, if you must know, it was yesterday. When we went riding. I told him then.'

Ashley gazed at him. 'But why? Why should you tell him that, Hussein?' She was appalled.

The boy hung his head. 'Why should I not tell him?' he demanded. 'It is true. I know Uncle Tariq likes you. Everybody likes you, even Muhammed!'

Ashley caught her breath. 'But you had no reason——'

'I had. I had!' Hussein looked up at her resentfully. 'It was awful yesterday, after you had your accident. Uncle Alain was so silent—so angry! He seemed to blame me for what had happened, and it was not my fault.' He sniffed. 'He was so concerned about you. He did not really want to continue with our ride at all.' He sighed. 'So I told him not to worry, that Uncle Tariq was at the palace to look after you.'

'Hussein!' Ashley could only articulate his name, and the boy stared at her in troubled defiance.

'Well!' he said, by way of justification. 'It was not your place to come with us. And falling off—you spoiled it all!'

Ashley forced herself to eat some lunch, simply because she knew if she didn't, she might not have the physical strength to do what she had to do. Hussein's words seemed to have sounded the death-knell for any hopes she had nurtured, and she had no doubt now that Alain's actions the night before had been prompted by what the boy had told him. Perhaps he saw her relationship with

Tariq as a mirror reflection of her association with Hassan, and despite his contempt for her, he had needed to prove to himself that he could still have her if he wanted. It was an ugly conclusion, but one which seemed to fit the circumstances, and Ashley knew a bitter disillusionment for having admitted it at last. They had defeated her. The Gauthier family had defeated her once again; and this time they had had her son's assistance.

When Nuzab came to take away her dirty dishes, Ashley asked how she might arrange an interview with Alain's father.

'You wish to see Prince Ahmed?' the Arab girl exclaimed in some surprise. 'But, *mademoiselle*, you cannot ask to see the Prince, he must ask to see you.'

Ashley sighed. 'Find Muhammed,' she said. 'Ask him. Tell him I must see Prince Ahmed today, and that it can't wait until tomorrow.'

Nuzab was forced to obey, but she looked somewhat anxious at the presumption of her mission. Somehow she identified herself with the wishes of her mistress, and making such a request was alien to her nature.

Nevertheless, when she returned some time later, it was with the news that Prince Ahmed had agreed to see Ashley at six o'clock. 'I spoke with Muhammed, as you said, lady,' she declared, still looking somewhat uneasy, and Ashley realised, with resignation, that Alain would no doubt hear of her request from him. But at least the interview was arranged, and Prince Ahmed could only approve of her decision.

Hussein—well, Hussein would only miss her momentarily. One thing she had proved by coming here, and that was that her son was quite content without her. Maybe if he had been brought up in England, the gulf between them would not have been so great. As it was, Alain was the real fulcrum of his world. He was his father's son. And in this country where man was always the master, he would take his place without any difficulty because of that.

Ashley spent the rest of the afternoon in a state of mild

panic, convinced that when Alain learned what she had arranged, as he surely would from Muhammed, he would come to find out what was going on. But the dusty heat of the day gave way to the cooler shadows of early evening, and no one disturbed her solitude. She would even have welcomed Nuzab's inconsequential chatter by the time the Arab girl appeared to escort her to Prince Ahmed's apartments, but for once the girl was silent and subdued, evidently still afraid her mistress's actions might recoil on her.

This time, when Ashley was shown into her father-in-law's rooms, he was alone. Neither Alain nor Muhammed were present, and even the two guards were bidden to wait beyond the heavy embossed doors.

As before, Prince Ahmed was seated at her entrance, but when he bade Ashley join him, she said she preferred to stand. It was not much of an advantage, but it was the only one she had, and besides, this wouldn't take long.

'So,' prompted her old enemy pointedly, 'to what purpose do you ask to see me, Miss Gilbert? Are your apartments not to your liking, perhaps? Or is my grandson not responding to the effeminate softness of your teaching?'

'Neither one of those things,' retorted Ashley tautly, refusing to abase herself by addressing him as *Prince*. 'My rooms are more than adequate for an English governess, and Hussein is an intelligent child, and progresses accordingly.'

'Then what possible reason can you have for wishing to speak with me?' demanded Prince Ahmed coldly. '*Mademoiselle*, I have guests at the palace—my old friend Prince Khalil and his daughter. I do not really have the time to waste over matters of minor importance, and I suggest you speak to Muhammed if all you require is conversation.'

Ashley's lips tightened, but she did not give in to the impulse to slap his cold arrogant face. Such behaviour might well land her in the palace's dungeons, she thought without humour, and quickly hastened into the reasons for this interview.

'I wish to leave, *monsieur*,' she declared through lips that persistently quivered, and for once Alain's father was too shocked to object to the familiarity.

'You wish to leave?' he echoed, and she knew a moment's triumph at her petty victory. 'But—but you cannot!' He gathered his composure with difficulty. 'No one—no one asks to leave the palace!'

'I am,' said Ashley flatly. 'I'd like to leave tomorrow, if that's possible. You don't have to worry about my salary—I'll waive that in lieu of notice. I just want to be on tomorrow's plane for London, and I'd like you to arrange it.'

Prince Ahmed got to his feet then, and Ashley saw without surprise that he was as tall as Alain. But whereas Alain's body was lean and muscular, his father's was thin and flabby, and somehow pathetic too as he sought to retain his dignity.

'Might one ask why you have come to this decision?' he asked, standing before her, and Ashley realised it was the first time he had spoken to her without an edge of contempt to his voice.

'I realised you were right,' she said after a moment. 'Alain was right—Hussein doesn't need me. He never did. And I was a fool to think I could be happy with anything less than the truth.'

Prince Ahmed's dark brows arched. 'The truth, *mademoiselle*?'

'Yes, the truth,' Ashley nodded. 'I've realised if I stay here, I'll lose what little self-respect I have. I thought I could do it, but I can't. So—I'm giving in. You've won.'

Prince Ahmed expelled his breath on a heavy sigh. 'I see.'

Ashley moistened her lips. 'I thought you would be pleased.'

'I am, of course.' The old man frowned. 'But I am sorry Alain was wrong about you. When you came here, he thought you had spirit.'

Ashley gasped. 'Spirit?'

'Yes.' He inclined his head. 'I could almost admire

that. Despite the fact that your intrusion into our lives was not of my choosing.'

Ashley shrugged. 'It seemed a good idea. Now I know it's no use.'

'So you are leaving?'

'Yes.'

'Have you told Alain?'

'No.'

'Why not?' Prince Ahmed hesitated. 'I should have thought you would have had plenty of time last night.'

'Last night?'

Ashley's face burned, and Prince Ahmed's features resumed their forbidding aspect. 'Please, do not attempt to lie to me, Miss Gilbert,' he said harshly. 'Do you think such a thing could happen in the palace without my becoming aware of it? I guessed where my son was the minute it was discovered he was absent from his apartments.' He paused. 'And I think it is that, and not my grandson, which threatens your self-respect!'

Ashley flinched. 'And you—condone your son's behaviour, *monsieur*?'

'So long as it does not interfere with my plans for Alain, why should I object if he chooses to make use of you, Miss Gilbert?' And at her gasp of horror he added: 'I trust him not to make the same mistakes a second time, *mademoiselle*. And I have usually found that that which is forbidden generally tastes sweetest. Why else do you think I permitted the marriage between you and Hassan?'

Ashley was trembling so much she could hardly keep her feet. 'You know so much, *monsieur*,' she exclaimed bitterly. 'So why didn't you know your younger son was impotent?'

'I did know.'

Ashley sought the support of a couch close by. Prince Ahmed's words had fallen like stones into a silent pool, the ripples deepening and widening with ever-increasing strength. She could hear her own heart beating, like a hammer against her temples, and a wave of senseless blackness advanced and retreated.

Perhaps Prince Ahmed noticed how pale she had suddenly become. Perhaps he knew a moment's compunction for the callousness of his statement. Whatever the truth of his feelings, he seemed to realise he had gone too far, and with a sound of impatience he hastened to retrieve the situation.

'I think I have been—a little indiscreet, *mademoiselle*,' he declared stiffly. 'Naturally, as Hassan's father I was aware of—some difficulty in that quarter——'

'Some difficulty!' Ashley could scarcely articulate the words. '*Monsieur*, you must know Hussein can't be Hassan's son!'

'I know no such thing,' retorted the old man harshly. 'You were married to Hassan, *mademoiselle*. Naturally, Hussein is the son of that marriage——'

'That's crazy!' Ashley stared at him incensed. 'Oh, this is inhuman! You must know Hassan could never father a child! Why do you think he drove his car into a tree, *monsieur*? Because he knew he could never be any good to any woman!'

'*No!*'

Yes.' Ashley was adamant. The feeling of faintness had receded and in its place was a tearful determination, but without this man's help she had no more hope of convincing Alain now than she had ever had. 'Please—can't you see what you're doing? You're denying your grandson his birthright! Hussein is Alain's son! You know that's true!'

'I know only that your influence divided this family, *mademoiselle*, and ultimately destroyed it!' Prince Ahmed stated grimly. 'Why do you think I sent Hassan to London? Because——'

'*You* sent Hassan to London?' Ashley interrupted blankly, and the old man nodded impatiently.

'Of course. Alain had spoken with his mother on the telephone. He told her of you, of your relationship. It was not a relationship I could ever condone.'

'But——'

'Alain is my eldest son,' declared her father-in-law proudly. 'I would not permit my eldest son to marry with an Englishwoman!'

'But you married a Frenchwoman.'

'Only when my first wife seemed incapable of producing a son.' His harsh features twisted. 'Alain is different. Alain is a Christian, thanks to his mother's influence. In consequence, he will take only one wife, and that wife could not be you, *mademoiselle*.'

Ashley swallowed convulsively. 'And—and Hassan was a Moslem.'

'That is correct.'

Ashley felt sick. 'So you—sent Hassan to London——'

'—to break up your relationship with Alain, yes. It was easier than I imagined. Hassan was foolish enough to fall in love with you.'

Ashley turned away. 'Does Alain know any of this?'

'As much as I deemed it necessary for him to know.'

'Which was?'

'He guessed Hassan's appearance in London was my doing. What he could not have anticipated was that you would find Hassan so attractive.'

'That's not true.' Ashley caught her breath. 'Hassan pursued me! Whenever Alain was out of the room, he—he tried to kiss me. He even tricked me into going to the apartment when Alain was not there.'

'But Alain turned up, did he not?' asked Prince Ahmed contemptuously. 'And found you in bed with Hassan!'

'No! No, it wasn't like that. I—Hassan put something in my drink. I was dizzy and I had to lie down. He carried me into the bedroom——'

'Please, do not go on.' The old man's features showed distaste now. 'I have no wish to hear such sordid details. It is enough that Alain realised the kind of girl you were before he made an irretrievable mistake.'

Ashley shook her head. 'But *you* know Hassan never touched me. You know he couldn't have fathered my child.'

'How else could I gain control of my grandson, except by acknowledging him as Hassan's son?' asked Prince Ahmed, with chilling rationality, and Ashley realised at last why he would never acknowledge Hussein as Alain's son. To do so would prove that Ashley was innocent, and remove the obstacles that stood between them.

Breathing deeply, to restore her shattered confidence, Ashley made one final plea. 'What if I go to Alain?' she cried. 'What if I tell him what you've just told me?'

'You are welcome to try, of course.' Prince Ahmed was supremely confident. 'But why should he believe you? He did not believe you before, did he?' He smiled, but it was not a friendly salutation. 'I shall deny everything, naturally.'

Ashley's shoulders sagged. 'So—you tricked me——'

'—into giving up your son?' Prince Ahmed snorted. 'What could you have done for him?'

'You pretended I had been paid off.'

'The money was there. If you chose not to take it . . .'

'I wanted nothing from you, nothing!' Ashley was vehement.

'And now?'

Ashley expelled her breath wearily. 'I just want to leave here. I never want to see any of you ever again.'

'Including your son?'

'He's not my son any more,' said Ashley heavily. 'You've seen to that. You—and Alain.'

'He is happy,' retorted her father-in-law indifferently. 'You cannot deny that.'

'No.' Ashley conceded defeat. 'No, I cannot deny that.'

'*Eh bien*,' he shrugged. 'I will make the necessary arrangements. A car will be made available to take you to the airport at six o'clock tomorrow evening. You will board the seven-thirty flight to London.'

The words 'Thank you' stuck in Ashley's throat. How could she thank him when he had successfully cheated her of the only man she had ever loved? If only she had not played his game! If only she had not married Hassan out of spite, to gain a father for her unborn son. If only Alain had had more faith in her, and less loyalty towards his brother . . .

CHAPTER TWELVE

ASHLEY tossed and turned until the early hours, alternately longing for or dreading the day ahead. She wanted to leave the palace, that much was certain, but the finality of what she was doing filled her with despair. Once she set foot on the plane to London she would never see Alain or her son again, and while her brain told her it was the only solution, her emotional responses answered differently. Wasn't she just playing into Prince Ahmed's hands once again? she asked herself. Wasn't she surrendering to his emotional blackmail? But how could she stay here, knowing he knew the truth, and compound it by living a lie?

The silken sheets on the huge bed had been changed, but Ashley could still sense Alain's occupancy. The scent of his body was still strong in her nostrils, the taste of his skin still sweet on her lips. Oh God, she thought bitterly, burying her face in the pillow, how was she going to exist without his love?

Nuzab packed Ashley's belongings the following morning with evident reluctance. It was obvious she did not approve of her mistress's hasty flight, and after wrapping some tissue paper round a pair of shoes, she turned to Ashley with troubled insistence.

'Lady not angry with Nuzab for what she saw yesterday?' she ventured, holding the tissue-swathed parcel against her like a shield. 'Nuzab say Prince Ahmed wish for Prince Alain to marry Princess Ramira, but not that Prince Alain wish it, too.'

Ashley sighed, taking pity on the girl. 'Don't worry, Nazab,' she said. 'It's not your fault. It's better that I go, honestly. It—it was a mistake to come here.'

'A mistake, lady?' Nuzab looked confused and Ashley realised how difficult it was for the Arab girl to understand her point of view, particularly when she didn't know the facts.

'I—I thought I'd like working in a foreign country,' she explained carefully, 'but I don't. I miss London. I'm sorry, Nuzab, you've been very kind to me, but I can't stay here.'

The Arab girl pursed her lips. 'It *is* Prince Alain, is it not?' she exclaimed suddenly. 'He has—how do you say it?—spoiled things ——'

'Oh, Nuzab!'

'It is true!' The Arab girl could see the unwilling acknowledgement in Ashley's eyes. 'He has made things—difficult for you, now?' She licked her lips. 'You do not like him, lady?'

'Nuzab——'

But Nuzab was shaking her head with evident astonishment. 'Prince Alain,' she was saying, almost inaudibly. 'Most women would consider themselves most fortunate if he chose to give them his favours.'

Ashley's lips tightened. 'Most Arab women,' she corrected tautly. 'Nuzab, I don't want to talk about it any more. Let it rest, will you?' She paused. 'Did you give Muhammed my message?'

'Yes, lady.' Nuzab was a little sullen now. 'He say the young Prince will miss you.'

Ashley had a struggle to keep her emotions in check, but she succeeded, and managed to say, almost carelessly: 'He'll soon forget me. I was only his governess, after all.'

This last was said with a note of bitterness, but Nuzab did not notice. 'My lady, Princess Hélène, say it is good for Prince Hussein to have a female tutor,' she declared severely. 'She say you have much affection for him.'

'I don't want to hear what Princess Hélène said!' retorted Ashley huskily. 'Please, Nuzab! Just do the packing. I'm going to take a shower.'

During the long afternoon, she was tempted to send a message to Alain, to notify him of what she was doing, just in case he had not been informed. But she could not believe that Muhammed would not have related the news

to his master at the earliest possible opportunity, and if
Alain chose not to come and see her, how could she risk
the chance of humiliating herself once again by sending
for him? He might not come. He might be busy entertain-
ing Princess Ramira, and Ashley's skin crawled at the
images her thoughts evoked. Images of Alain in another
woman's arms, sharing with her the rapturous consummation they had shared. She could not bear the thought
of the Arab girl's limbs entwined with his, her black hair
spread out upon his pillow. But she could not dismiss the
memory of the sensuous aftermath of passion, and Alain
lying, relaxed and lazily satiated, in *her* arms . . .

She put on the same black corded pants suit to travel
back to London that she had worn to come out here. For
once, she allowed her hair to remain unbound, securing it
at her nape with a leather thong, so that it cascaded
down her back like a fall of golden silk.

She was ready and waiting when the servant arrived to
escort her to the car, and although she knew a momentary compunction at not having bade goodbye to
Prince Ahmed's wives, she knew that if Hélène had been
kind to her, she might have broken down completely. It
was easier to say goodbye to neither of them than to
single one out for the dubious honour, and she had left
her apologies with Nuzab, to deliver after she was gone.

It was the same sleek limousine that had brought her
from the airport a little over two weeks ago that was
waiting in the courtyard, and Ashley had to steel herself
not to look back as she climbed inside. Was Alain standing behind one of those arched doorways, watching her
departure? Or had he taken it without dissension, too
absorbed in his new companion to pay any attention to
the withdrawal of a servant?

Only one guard accompanied her into the back of the
car, before the chauffeur set the vehicle in motion. He
was a dark-skinned Arab, with a scar on his left cheek,
and Ashley felt a little uneasy under his vaguely speculative gaze. It crossed her mind briefly that Prince Ahmed
might have some less welcome fate waiting for her then a

seat on the plane to London, but she quickly dismissed it as the imaginings of a frustrated libido.

They passed through the city of Khadesh, and Ashley looked sadly out at the floodlit buildings and formal squares. She had not even set foot in the city, and she leaned back against the leather upholstery, feeling unutterably weary.

Until now, she had managed to keep the thoughts of Hussein at bay, but now memories of her son came to torment her. Being with him, working with him, sharing a little of his life, had been her dream: but it had turned into a nightmare. She had been a fool to imagine she could roll back the events of seven years—his whole life, in fact—and begin again, as if those seven years had never been. She had read somewhere that a child's character was formed before he was seven years old. So far as Hussein was concerned, she had never existed—and never would.

Beyond Khadesh the road became very uneven, and Ashley was thrown about in her seat. She grasped the leather support that hung between the windows, and tried to stare out into the darkness, but all she could see was the limousine's headlights, and a rough and bumpy road ahead of them. She frowned. It was only a few days ago that she and Princess Hélène had driven along this road, and it hadn't been rough then. Could it really have deteriorated in such a short space of time, or was this not the road to the airport?

The panic she had briefly felt at the palace flowered anew. Who were these men? Where were they taking her? What awful scheme was this to prevent her from catching the plane? She should have written to Lucy, she thought impotently. As soon as she knew she was leaving, she should have written to her. As it was, no one but Prince Ahmed and a few servants knew she was leaving the palace, and it could be many weeks or months before her absence was reported.

With what she felt was extreme composure, she looked at the man opposite her. 'This is not the road to the airport, she said, hearing the revealing tremor in her voice. 'Where are you taking me? I want to know. By—by whose orders am I being kidnapped?'

She could not see the Arab's face in the darkness, but his shrug was an eloquent reflection of his indifference. Then, as a sense of horror gripped her, she forced her hysteria away. Of course, she told herself severely, he would not understand English. Few of the servants did. Unless she acted in blind terror, she would have to wait until they reached their destination to find out what they had in store for her.

By the time the lights of some settlement appeared ahead of them, Ashley's whole body was bathed in a cold sweat. She could not control her panic. It was an instinctive thing. And no matter how she tried, she could think of no innocent motive behind this silent abduction.

It was only as the car stopped, and the chauffeur came round to open her door, that Ashley realised they had been crossing the desert. Beneath her feet, the sand crunched alarmingly, and all about her were the unmistakable components of a desert encampment. There were tall tents and campfires, the aromatic flavour of meat roasting, and the disconcerting grunts from a group of camels.

Ashley's lips parted, as she avoided the chauffeur's hand and stared about her in amazement. But when her eyes at last darted upward to meet the man's dark gaze, she started in astonishment as she recognised her abductor.

'Muhammed!' she breathed, moving her head disbelievingly. 'Oh, Muhammed! I thought you were my friend.'

'I am your friend, *mademoiselle*,' retorted the tall Arab harshly, making a slight bow. 'Come—follow me. There is someone waiting to see you. A Bedouin encampment may not be as luxurious as a palace, but I think you will not be disappointed.'

'But, Muhammed——'

'Come!' he silenced her firmly, and with a helpless shake of her head, she followed him stumblingly across the rough ground. They passed several groups of people, gathered about their campfires, roasting meat for the evening meal. The firelight played across their faces as they watched Ashley's progress with dark enigmatic eyes, and it warmed her trembling legs as she struggled to keep up with her escort.

Muhammed took her to a larger than average pavilion, set slightly apart from the rest, and with a little flourish pulled aside the flap. His hand in the small of her back propelled her into the warm scented atmosphere within its canvas walls, and she gazed about her wonderingly at its luxurious appointments. Purple and gold hangings gave it the appearance of an opulent apartment in the palace, there were polished bronze lamps, and an en-amelled stove, that gave off a wave of heat, and a lushly-cushioned couch, strewn with satin covers, set squarely in the middle of the exotically patterned carpet. It was like something out of the Arabian Nights, and when Ashley glanced round and found she was alone, panic gripped her again. What was this, the tent of some white slaver? she wondered sickly, but before her fears could catapult her into action, a man appeared from behind a screen at the other side of the tent.

'*Oh, God!*'

To her ignominy, her legs refused to support her any longer, and with a little cry she collapsed on to the car-peted floor of the tent, shaking uncontrollably. Somehow, even though Muhammed had brought her here, Alain was the last person she had expected to see, and her last threads of composure vanished as he came irresistibly towards her.

He was wearing the djellaba, the loose robe that fell in folds of purple linen from his shoulders, but his head was bare. He epitomised the fascination of his father's an-cestry combined with the gentler sensitivity of his mother's blood, and when he knelt on one knee and gath-ered her into his arms, she had no strength left to deny him.

'Oh, Ashley,' he said, against her mouth, 'did you

really think I would let you run away from me?'

It was that word 'would' that brought Ashley briefly to her senses. Not 'could'—but 'would'; as if she had no say in the matter. With a choked sound of protest she thrust his arms away from her, and scrambling to her feet, she staggered towards the flap of the tent and freedom.

She had scarcely got two yards before his arms captured her from behind, drawing her resisting body back against him, laughing softly when she struggled to evade his questing lips. 'Stop fighting me, Ashley,' he commanded huskily. 'It is a losing battle, as I have found to my cost. I wanted to go on hating you, but I find that I need you, and contrary to my father's wishes, I *have* to forgive you!'

Ashley was still as his arms continued to hold her, her head throbbing from the effort to understand him. 'You—you have to forgive me?' she articulated with difficulty. 'I—I don't understand. Forgive me for what?'

Alain bent his head, his teeth moving against the soft skin of her neck. 'For marrying Hassan,' he declared roughly. 'For letting your resentment dictate your actions!'

Ashley stiffened then, twisting to escape him, but he would not let her go. 'Be still,' he said huskily, his hands sliding beneath the hem of her jacket. 'You are not going to leave here, until we leave together, so you might as well accept that in fact I am the master.'

'My master? *Never!*' exclaimed Ashley fiercely, though her strength had been drained by the emotional strains of the journey. 'Alain, I don't know why you've brought me here, what devious plan you have in mind. But I'm leaving Murad just as soon as I can get on board a plane, and nothing you can say or do will stop me!'

'Nothing?' he taunted softly, his hands sliding deliberately upward, to cup the revealing swell of her breasts through the fine material of her shirt. 'Oh, Ashley, your body betrays you! You want me just as much as I want you!'

With a swift movement he brought her round to face

him, and when she still would have resisted him, he imprisoned both her hands within one of his, behind her back. Then, with deliberate slowness, he unfastened the buttons of her jacket, his lips twisting sensuously when he viewed with satisfaction the pointed peaks outlined against the tautness of her shirt.

'I—I'll hate you for this!' she hissed, fighting the attraction he had for her almost as much as her attraction for him. 'Alain, why are you doing this? What do you want? I thought you'd be glad I was leaving.'

Alain's mouth curved. 'You know, six weeks ago I would have agreed with you,' he said, his voice deep and disturbing. 'Six weeks ago, when I brought Hussein to London. I knew I was taking a chance, but I believed myself capable of running that risk.'

Ashley's lips parted. 'You—expected to see me?'

Alain nodded. 'Oh, not at Brede School—that was a cruel irony. No, my intention was simply to visit you, to give you a report on Hussein's development, to reassure you that he was happy and content.'

Ashley gazed at him. 'But why? You had never done such a thing before.'

'No, this is true.' With a sudden groan, he propelled her closer. 'But right now I suspect my motives were not as detached as I would have liked to believe.'

'Alain——' With her thighs crushed against his legs, she could not help but be aware of the rugged strength of his body against her, and while the way he was holding her made her arms ache, her lower limbs yielded to other sensations.

'God, Ashley, I have got to do it,' he muttered, releasing her wrists suddenly, and her arms slid almost compulsively round his neck when his mouth took possession of hers.

The jacket of her suit fell heedlessly to the floor, to be followed seconds later by her shirt. He pressed it off her shoulders, his mouth seeking and finding the soft flesh now exposed to his gaze, and when he looked upon the rose-tipped fullness of her breasts, his blue eyes grew dark and caressing.

'Say that you want me,' he demanded, pushing her back on to the couch. 'Tell me you need me—that you cannot live without me, for as God is my witness, life without you has been hell indeed!'

The cushions were soft and satiny smooth to her bare skin, and Alain's taut body crushed her down into their yielding depths. He didn't seem to care that the tent flap was untied, or that Muhammed might return at any moment. He was totally absorbed in the process of giving her pleasure, and pleasing himself at the same time, and the urgent demands of passion drove all rational thought from Ashley's head.

'I want you, I want you,' she breathed, winding her arms about his neck, and arching her limbs to accommodate him. 'I love you, Alain, I always have. Oh, darling, *darling*, love me, too!'

Their lovemaking was a devastating experience for both of them, but when it was over, Alain did not move away from her as he had done before. Instead, he smoothed the strands of damp hair back from her forehead, and sought her mouth with his.

'My love,' he breathed, his hands sliding down her spine to the provocative curve of her hips, and she nodded her head energetically, still too bemused to say too much.

'I must be careful,' he said huskily, as she stirred sensuously against him. 'I might get you pregnant again, and for the present I prefer to keep you all to myself.'

Ashley's eyes widened disbelievingly. 'A-again?' she whispered, wondering if she had imagined the import of his statement, and Alain's lips played with her fluttering lashes.

'You told me Hussein was my son,' he reminded her softly. 'And for the present, I would rather not increase our family.'

Ashley's mouth was dry. 'Are—are you teasing me, Alain?'

'Why?' His teeth caught the lobe of her ear and

nibbled persuasively. 'Because I am prepared to accept what you say is true?'

'It is true!' Ashley spoke urgently. 'But do you really believe me? Or are you just—pretending?'

'Does this seem like pretence to you?' he demanded, his eyes narrowed and heavy with emotion. 'I believe you, Ashley. I believe you because I have to. Because if I look at Hussein honestly, without the distorted shades of jealousy, I can see that he resembles me more than he resembles Hassan.'

'And—and is that all?' asked Ashley tremulously.

'No.' Alain shook his head. 'No, it was something else, something that made me question my reasons for doubting you.'

'Which was?' She was anxious.

'The night I spent with you,' he said simply. 'The night I came to your apartments. The night when I discovered that I could not let you leave me again.' He sighed, burying his face in the hollow between her breasts, so that when he spoke again his voice was muffled. 'I have to ask you,' he muttered. 'Has there been another man? You can tell me. I can take it. Just—do not lie to me—ever.'

'There's been no other man,' she assured him honestly, and he gathered her closer against him.

'I knew it,' he groaned, cradling her face between his hands. 'Do not ask me how—but I knew it. That was when I started to believe what I had wanted to believe for so long.'

'You—wanted to believe it?' Ashley was confused.

'I suppose that was why I wanted to see you,' he admitted huskily. 'Living with Hussein, watching him grow, observing all the little mannerisms he has that reminded me of myself.' He lifted his head. 'I should ask you to forgive me.' He drew an unsteady breath. 'Why in God's name did you marry Hassan?'

'Because I was pregnant,' she answered unevenly. 'And—and I wanted to hurt you.'

'That you did,' he admitted with feeling. 'Dear God,

Ashley, I went through hell!'

Ashley looked into his blue eyes. 'Perhaps you deserved to,' she whispered, still not entirely convinced of his sincerity. 'You were prepared to believe the worst of me, always.'

Alain inclined his head with weary self-denigration. 'You are right, of course. But you must admit I had cause.'

'Finding me and Hassan on your bed?'

Alain's mouth tightened. 'And if it had been me—with some other woman?'

'I know, I know,' Ashley's slim arms wound her closer to him. 'Oh, Alain, hold me, hold me! I'm so afraid this won't last.'

'It will last,' he assured her thickly. 'But go on. I want to hear it all. I want us to have this conversation and then never speak of it again.'

'What do you want to know?'

'Everything.' His lips touched hers and then withdrew as the contact evoked other, more disturbing desires. 'What happened between you and Hassan? What did he tell you?'

'Only that you were likely to let me down,' she conceded reluctantly. 'That you had many girl-friends. That he was a much more stable character.'

Alain gazed at her. 'But how could you believe him?'

'I didn't,' replied Ashley simply. 'I wouldn't listen to him. But he was so—persistent. And—forward.' She sighed. 'He used to touch me, whenever he had the opportunity. Oh, Alain, I know he's dead, but he deliberately set out to break up our relationship!'

'I'm beginning to believe it.' Alain nodded. 'Go on.'

'The day—the day you found us at the apartment, I got a message, ostensibly from you. Like you often used to send—arranging that we should meet at the apartment. But when I got there, you weren't there, Hassan was. He—he said you'd been delayed, that we should have a drink while we waited.' She hesitated. 'I can't prove this, but I think he must have put something in my drink. I remember I felt very hot suddenly, and very dizzy.' She shivered involuntarily as the memory of what happened next returned to torment her, but Alain's arms were warm about her, his muscled body a protection against the chills of the past. 'Hassan—Hassan must have noticed how I was feeling. He probably *knew*! He—he suggested I should lie down for a while, and I agreed. I suppose you think that was very silly, but I didn't know what he had in mind.' She paused. 'Do you want me to go on?'

'Please.'

Alain's request was gentle, and with a trembling sigh she obeyed. 'Well, I lay on the bed. I—I do remember unloosening the neck of my dress because I was so hot! But the next thing I knew, Hassan had—had taken off his jacket, and his shirt, and was leaning over me, saying all sorts of wild things, like how much he admired me, and how much he wanted me, and that I was the only girl he had ever loved!' She swallowed convulsively. 'It was crazy! I knew he couldn't love me, and I couldn't believe it was happening. Then—then——'

'—I came,' Alain finished for her softly. 'Yes, I came. And we all know what happened after that.'

Ashley looked up at him anxiously. 'That's how it was, I swear to you,' she breathed, half afraid he would disbelieve her story even now. But Alain only bent his head and silenced her protesting mouth with his, and for a long time there was only the sound of their shaken breathing to disturb the stillness.

However, at last Alain recovered sufficiently to ask: 'When did you discover you were pregnant?'

'I already knew,' she confessed, stroking the curve of his cheek. 'I was going to tell you that afternoon. I—I was very apprehensive. I didn't know how you would take it.'

'How I would take it?' he muttered. 'You knew I loved you.'

'Yes. But I knew your family wouldn't—wouldn't approve of our relationship, and—and they didn't, did they?'

'I make my own decisions,' declared Alain roughly. 'Nothing and no one would have prevented me from marrying you.'

Ashley nodded. 'I—I wanted to believe that.'

'God!' Alain pressed his face into the silken curtain of her hair. 'If Hassan were still alive——'

'But he's not,' Ashley whispered softly. 'We—we must learn to forgive Hassan.'

'He has deprived us of seven years!' exclaimed Alain harshly.

'We'll have many more,' insisted Ashley huskily. 'Oh, darling, don't be bitter. Not now.'

'How can you say that?' he demanded. 'If only I had not been so blind, so stubborn, so utterly jealous!'

Ashley expelled her breath shakily. 'And now?'

'Now I am going to marry you,' he said fiercely. 'And no one will stop me.'

'And—and Hussein?'

'Hussein will be told the truth,' said Alain simply. 'Oh, maybe not yet. It may be too much for him to take all at once.'

'He—he'll resent me.'

'Perhaps.' Alain knew there was no point in minimising the difficulties. 'But he will get over that. And perhaps when he learns he is in truth my son——'

'He'll never forgive me,' Ashley insisted unsteadily.

'He will if I tell him how it was,' declared Alain gently. 'Do not worry, darling. Hussein will not blame you. I will see to it.'

Ashley was still anxious, but perhaps Alain was right. The boy was still young. He might learn to forgive both of them. And they had all the time in the world to make it right.

'How did you know I was leaving?' she asked suddenly. 'Did Muhammed tell you?'

'But of course.' Alain smiled and rolled on to his back, and Ashley pillowed her head on his broad chest. 'Do you know he is your most faithful ally? I left you in his care when I went away.'

Ashley bit her lip. 'Did he also tell you about Tariq?'

Alain shifted so that he could see her face. 'My little brother? Oh, yes, he told me.'

'Hussein told you, too, didn't he?'

Alain's eyes were amused. 'You thought I might believe that Tariq had taken Hassan's place?'

Ashley coloured. 'Were you jealous?'

Alain's eyes darkened. 'A little.'

'You didn't think——'

'——that you were interested in him? No.' He pushed his fingers through her silky hair. 'I was learning to trust you, and not myself.'

'Oh, Alain! I can't believe this . . .'

'Can you not?' He pulled her across him, his hands in the small of her back pressing her close to him. 'Is this not real enough for you? Do you want further proof?'

'Oh, Alain . . .'

Her lips had descended to his to play sensuously with his mouth, when Muhammed's voice hailed them from outside the tent.

'Prince Alain! Prince Alain!' he called insistently. '*Mademoiselle*, my master has a visitor.'

'A visitor?'

Ashley gulped, and with a groan of impatience Alain reached for a rug of skins to draw over them. Then, when Ashley would have pulled away from him, he imprisoned her within the curve of his arm, tucking the rug securely over her breasts.

'Come!' he called, and then released her to sit upright when his mother walked into the pavilion ahead of Muhammed.

Princess Hélène was almost unidentifiable in a cloak of soft sable, but her eyes were bright and inquisitive, and remarkably unsurprised to find Ashley with her son. At his mother's entrance, however, Alain uttered a muffled oath, and with a word of apology to Ashley he slid from the couch, accepting the dark robe Muhammed offered him to wrap around his naked body.

'This is an honour, *madame*,' he remarked, with mild

asperity, and his mother grimaced at his evident sarcasm.

'An unnecessary one, obviously,' she said, smiling more kindly at Ashley. 'Do you know you have had me driving half around the country?'

Alain drew a deep breath and folded his arms. 'Really?'

'Yes, really.' Princess Hélène waved Ashley to remain where she was as the girl shifted with some embarrassment. 'I was so afraid Ashley would take the plane, and I had so little time to prevent her.'

'To prevent me, *madame*?' Ashley wriggled up on the cushions, glancing anxiously across at Alain.

'Yes, *chérie*,' declared Princess Hélène firmly. 'Alain, do you have a drink for a weary traveller? Some coffee, perhaps? Or some tea? Or even a glass of lemon juice to take the taste of sand out of my mouth.'

'But how did you find us, *madame*?' exclaimed Ashley, as Alain bade Muhammed bring some coffee, and Princess Hélène seated herself conspiratorially on the end of the couch.

'I knew Alain must be here,' she explained, ignoring her son's taut features. 'These are his father's people, and he has always been a favourite with them.'

'This is Numara,' Alain added, by way of an explanation. 'Where I was going to take you the morning we went riding,' and Ashley's limbs melted beneath the fiery possession in his eyes when he looked at her.

'Where you are is not important, *chérie*,' Princess Hélène continued half impatiently. 'What was important was that I should speak to you—to both of you,' she glanced up at her son again, 'and remove any doubts from Alain's mind that Hussein is not his son.'

Alain's gaze transferred itself to his mother, and Ashley's lips parted in sudden apprehension. What was Princess Hélène going to say? After all that had happened, Ashley was so afraid she might spoil things.

'I do not understand, Maman.' Alain came down on his haunches beside his mother. 'What can you possibly tell me that I do not know already? I should explain—I have told Ashley that I believe her, that I accept her story. There is no need to labour the point.'

'Oh, but there is.' Hélène turned back to Ashley. 'My dear child, I know what you went through yesterday evening.'

Ashley's colour darkened, and then receded. 'You— *know!*'

'About your interview with my husband? But of course. He thinks he is the only one in the palace with spies, but he is wrong. I, too, have my methods of finding out those things that I wish to know, and when I learned that you had asked for an interview with my husband, I was curious to know why.'

'But who——'

'Nuzab, of course. She was most concerned about you, too. It was she who delivered the news of your departure, as you had asked, and without her assistance I could not have attempted to stop you.'

'To stop me, *madame?*'

'From leaving,' explained Hélène, putting out a hand and pressing her son's taut shoulder. 'Darling, do not look so severe,' she exclaimed. 'Surely if you have told Ashley you believe her, she has told you of the interview she had with Prince Ahmed last evening!'

'No.' Alain's mouth was stern. 'No, she has told me nothing. What is there to tell?'

'Oh, Alain . . .' Ashley pushed her fingers into her hair, sensing the depth of his frustration. 'Darling, it was nothing. Nothing. It doesn't matter now. Not now we're together.'

'How can you say so?' Hélène turned to her son. 'Alain, your father knew of Hassan's impotency when he sent him to London!'

'What!'

'It is true.' Hélène spread her hands. 'Oh, these things are common knowledge among the women of the household. Need I explain? There were girls—servant girls— who tried to please him, you understand? But it was no use.'

'And my father *sent* him to London?'

'Alain——'

Ashley tried to intervene, but Hélène wouldn't let her. 'To break up your friendship with Ashley,' she agreed. 'Because you were his eldest son, his heir, and a Christian into the bargain.'

'My God!' Alain rose abruptly to his feet, and Ashley had never seen him look so incensed. 'I should kill him!'

'What? Kill your own father?' Hélène rose now, fluttering her hands in sudden anxiety. 'Alain, Alain, I did not tell you this for you to threaten your father's life. He is my husband, and for all his faults, I still love him, God forgive me. But it had to be told. Ashley was an innocent pawn in your father's game.'

Alain took several minutes to digest what his mother had just told him, and in the meantime Muhammed returned with a tray of coffee. Alain bade him set it down, then turned abruptly to Ashley.

'And you knew all this?' he demanded. Then, when she nodded, he exclaimed: 'Why did you not tell me?'

Ashley sighed. 'Would you have believed me?'

Alain's face assumed a little darkening colour. 'A fair question,' he muttered savagely and then, with sudden vehemance, he squatted down beside her again, and ignoring his mother and Muhammed cupped her pale face between his hands.

'I do not know how, but *somehow* I will make up to you for this,' he stated harshly. 'I have been a fool, and an arrogant one, and I do not deserve your love. But believe me when I tell you no one else will ever part us—ever! You have my word on that.'

Ashley was trembling when he had finished, and she could tell by his eyes that he wanted nothing so much as to gather her into his arms there and then. But he had some regard for his mother's sensitivities, and after bestowing a lingering kiss on Ashley's parted lips, he rose to his feet once more.

'I have not thanked you, Maman, for delivering this information,' he said, his voice clipped and constrained, and his mother sighed.

'Dare I say I am glad it was not necessary?' she ventured. 'Alain, when did you begin to suspect the truth?'

Her son's shoulders sagged, as he endeavoured to relax. 'I do not know,' he said, running a weary hand over his eyes. 'Two, maybe three years ago, I began to notice certain things aout Hussein. But it was not until Muhammed also made the comparison that I realised that perhaps I had been wrong.'

'Oh, *chéri!*' His mother caught his hand, raising it to her lips. '*Chéri*, do not be too bitter.' She glanced round at Ashley. 'You are young, you will have other children. And you know your father has much affection for his grandchildren, despite the fact that he seldom shows it.'

Alain shook his head. 'You know, I used to wonder why my father wanted me to believe that Hussein was Hassan's son. Now I know. If I had ever suspected the truth, I might have come looking for Ashley. Even believing that she and Hassan had been lovers, he knew I might still have wanted her . . .'

Princess Hélène sighed. 'Let it go. He let you bring Ashley here, did he not?'

'Because he was afraid if he refused, Ashley might make waves,' retorted Alain tautly. 'I can see it all now. He was afraid it might all come out again.'

'As it has,' pointed out his mother dryly. 'Alain, *chéri*, your father is an old man, and you are his eldest son! He wanted you to marry someone of his race and creed. Only he forgot—your will is as strong as his.'

Alain expelled his breath heavily. 'How did you know you would find Ashley here?' he asked, trying to relieve the tense atmosphere that had developed, and his mother smiled again.

'I did not—at least, not at first. I went to the airport, and when I found that she had not checked in for the flight to London, I made my own calculation.'

Alain's hard mouth softened a little. 'Well, as you can see, she is safe and sound.'

'Is she?' Princess Hélène's brows arched flirtatiously. 'Well, sound anyway. When will you come back to the palace?'

Alain sighed. 'The way I feel right now, I do not think I ever want to see my father again.'

'But you will.' His mother was anxious.

'Maybe. Some day.' Alain was noncommittal. 'After I have spent a couple of years in New York, then perhaps I will be able to face him again with equanimity.'

'New York?'

'New York?'

Ashley and Hélène spoke simultaneously, but it was to the girl on the couch Alain addressed his reply. 'If you are willing,' he said, squatting beside her again. 'This appointment the government of Murad offered me—it is still open. I think I should take it, do you?'

Ashley hesitated. 'And—Hussein?'

'He will come with us, of course.'

'Oh, Alain!' His mother sounded distressed.

'It is the only way,' said her son with finality. 'It will be good for all of us to get away from the cloying influence of the palace. In two years' time, when we come back, the past will be behind us. And perhaps by then my father will have learned not to interfere in other people's lives!'

Ashley touched his cheek. 'If it's what you want.'

'It is what I want,' Alain agreed huskily. 'Do you not know the only reason I turned down that appointment in New York was because I could not bear to leave you behind?'

Princess Hélène rose to her feet. 'I think it is time I left,' she said, but her eyes were twinkling as she bent to kiss her son's cheek. 'Look after him, Ashley,' she added. 'I know you will. I knew it the moment I saw you.'

The dinner party was over, and Ashley walked into the large bedroom she shared with Alain, hiding a yawn behind her hand. Her husband had preceded her, leaving her to turn out the lights before joining him, and now she saw him standing on the balcony outside their bedroom windows, looking over the panorama of the East River spread out below them. Although it was late, the river was a mass of lights, the mournful sound of a ship's siren drifting to her ears.

It was six months since they had come to New York, six months since their marriage in Paris, and their subsequent honeymoon on the island of Antigua, and the time seemed to have flown. Ashley had never been so happy, or so content, and even her relationship with Hussein was less one-sided than it used to be. Oh, he had resented her, that son of hers, using every method in the book to discredit her in Alain's eyes. But Alain had learned his lesson well from more sophisticated hands than those of his son, and as the days turned into weeks and the weeks into months, and it became obvious that nothing could shake his love for Ashley, Hussein was learning to admit defeat gracefully.

Muhammed had been a great help. He had accompanied them to New York, much to Ashley's delight and relief, and it was he who was gradually weaning the boy to the idea that it was not half bad having a mother and a father. Hussein had taken the news of his relationship to Alain with great excitement, but so far his reaction to Ashley's involvement in his creation had been lukewarm. But it would come, she was sure of it. And perhaps, in a few months' time . . .

Flexing her shoulder muscles lazily, she crossed the softly piled carpet and leaned against the open french doors. 'Darling,' she murmured, 'will you unzip me?' and Alain turned from his contemplation of the city to view his wife with tender loving eyes.

'Better than that, I will undress you, if you would like me to,' he breathed, his mouth finding her soft shoulder. 'You were magnificent this evening, do you know that? My father was proud of you, I could tell.'

Ashley grimaced as the silky sheath fell away, revealing her slender figure in a long virginally white slip. 'Do you think so?' she asked anxiously. 'Do you really think so? Are you sure he wasn't just being polite because he wants you to forgive him?'

'That, too, of course,' agreed Alain, with amused cyni-

cism, as her hands sought the cord of his bathrobe. 'But
you handled those delegates from the United Nations as if
you had been born to the task, and I could see the old
man preening in the light of their admiration for his
daughter-in-law.'

'Oh, Alain, I hope so.' Ashley pressed herself closer,
and Alain's fingers expertly slid aside the straps of her
slip.

'I know so,' he said huskily, his hands seeking and finding her breasts. 'He came to New York to conciliate, and
he finds he is actually pleased at the way things are
going.'

Ashley sighed, sliding her arms around his neck. 'I
liked your friends the Fareins. Did you say they lived in
Cairo?'

'Hmm.' Alain was loosening her hair from its knot,
letting it fall about her shoulders. 'Do you remember,
they were the family I once tried to persuade you to take
a position with. But you turned me down.'

Ashley drew back to look at him. 'Oh, yes.' She
frowned. 'Why did you do that?'

Alain grimaced. 'Can you not guess? I had some idea
of visiting the Fareins and seeing you again, without your
really being aware of it. I was so confused at that time. I
just knew I had to see you again.'

Ashley smiled. 'Oh, darling! That makes what I have
to tell you that much easier.'

'What you have to tell me?' Alain looked puzzled.
'What is it?'

Ashley hesitated. 'I'm pregnant. I—I wasn't sure until
today, but I saw Dr Raphael this after——'

She didn't finish. Alain's mouth had captured hers,
and his urgent possession made her weak with longing for
him. There was no censure in his kiss, only an overwhelming passion, and her senses spun beneath the prob-
ing caress of his mouth.

'When?' he asked at last, when he let her get her
breath, and her tongue appeared in unknowing provocation.

'In about thirty weeks,' she replied, after a moment's hesitation. 'You don't mind? You're not angry?'

'Well, since it has already happened it's a little late for me to object now' he whispered, with wry humour. 'Oh, darling, of course I do not mind. I can think of nothing more satisfying than looking at you and seeing you grow big with my child.'

'Alain!'

'Do I shock you?' His lips teased. 'Ashley, you had our first child without my love and support. Be assured that will never happen again.'

And he took pains to prove it.

SUPERROMANCE
SUBSCRIPTION
RESERVATION COUPON

Complete and mail TODAY to

Harlequin Reader Service

In the U.S.A.
1440 South Priest Drive
Tempe, AZ 85281

In Canada
649 Ontario Street
Stratford, Ontario N5A 6W2

Please reserve my subscription to the 2 NEW
SUPERROMANCES published every eight weeks
(12 a year). Every eight weeks I will receive
2 NEW SUPERROMANCES at the low price of
$2.50 each (total— $5). There are no shipping and
handling or any other hidden charges, and I am free
to cancel at any time after taking as many or
as few novels as I wish.

MY PRESENT SUBSCRIPTION NUMBER IS_____

NAME_____
            (Please Print)

ADDRESS_____

CITY_____

STATE/PROV._____

ZIP/POSTAL CODE_____